A NOVEL OF IMPORTANCE

The World According To GUS

OTHER BOOKS BY JOSEPH M. BERNARD

AWAKEN:
100 Questions To Expand Your Mind and Open Your Heart

FINDING THE VOICE OF THE SOUL:
A Bold Path Inviting Consciousness and Compassion

THE

A NOVEL OF IMPORTANCE

World

ACCORDING TO

Gus

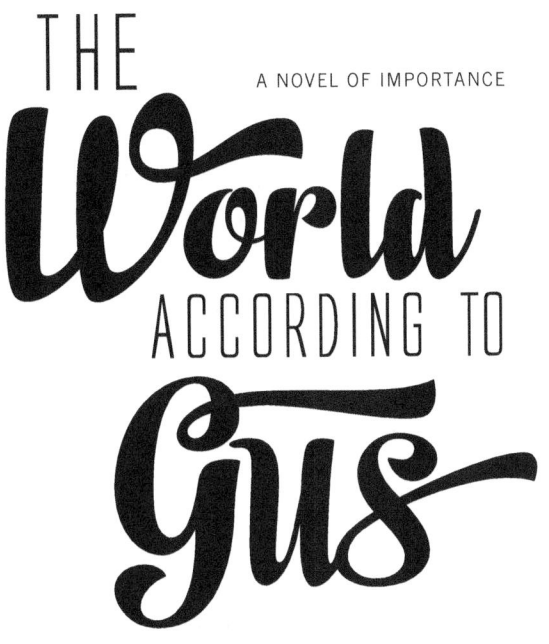

JOSEPH M. BERNARD

Wee
ginger
Press

ISBN: 978-0-9960785-9-7

Wild Ginger Press
www.wildgingerpress.com

CONTENTS

PART I

GUS Sets the Record Straight   1

PART 2

The Blog According to GUS   97

PART 3

The Mass Awakening   135

PART 4

The Healing Story   177

To all those who venture down the path of discovering their own truth. It is a courageous journey.

ACKNOWLEDGMENTS

Thank you to my wife Bobbi, for the beautiful design of the cover and content for this book, and for her work to make it the best book it could be.

Thank you to my sister Joan, who read it initially and assisted with the editing. She helped me move forward and now she gets to see the results of our efforts.

Thank you, Johnni Prince, who did the final extensive edit. With Johnni's great help the book flows more smoothly making it a better read.

*Reexamine all that you have been told
in school, or in church, or in any book.
Dismiss whatever insults your soul.*

~ WALT WHITMAN

AUTHOR'S NOTE

The idea for this book happened in a flash of inspiration and within an hour I had a full outline. This story came to me in a flow of words and ideas, and represents no religious point of view. I did my best to simply get out of the way and let the story be told as my fingers worked away.

As you read this book, I am sure you will feel the wisdom and compassion of something much more powerful than me at work. Please take the words of this higher voice that called itself "God" (until that changed) and let them in, so that you can sense what feels true to you.

As you read along you will see "I Am" often. These are the words of God and this short phrase is capitalized throughout the book for two reasons. One reason for the "I Am" is to remind you that "God" is speaking and that it is time to focus and pay attention. The second reason is that "I Am" is a powerful statement of the Divine nature in every human being. When "God" says, "I Am", "God" is reminding you of your unity with the source of all creation.

In this book "God" never speaks in conjunctions (can't, won't, wasn't, etc.) because, again, "God" wants you to slow down and tune into what is being said.

Now, free yourself of any limiting ideas or beliefs that you may have held in the past and carefully listen to the messages contained in this story. They are presented to you so that you might open your heart and mind to all that this divine voice has to say. Please enjoy, explore and let yourself be uplifted by these words full of hope and human possibilities.

Joseph M. Bernard, PhD.
Winter 2014

PREFACE

I am here to tell you about an extraordinary experience that happened to a seemingly ordinary man. In actual fact, there was nothing ordinary about it at all.

The man's name is Fred Jacobs and this story is about the experience he had that forever changed his life. He is inspired to share his story because he thinks it just might do the same for you.

Fred lives in Portland, Oregon where he writes for the local newspaper and his main beat is covering professional basketball. The Portland fans are incredibly dedicated even though professional basketball teams have a kind of roller coaster existence, with good times and not-so-good times. In that way, sports are much like life, with their ups and downs.

This story however, is not about sports, but Fred feels it is necessary to tell you where he comes from so you can understand how different his life became as this story unfolds.

He is a middle-aged guy who recently separated from Jenny, his wife of over 20 years. She told him that things were just not working and she thought they needed to be apart to sort things out. Fred was surprised by her decision because he had no idea that things were that bad between them.

He admitted to being emotionally out of touch sometimes.

He just thought that since they loved each other that was all that mattered.

When he moved out they both cried. Fred couldn't remember the last time he'd done that. It was a day filled with sadness for him. His emotions were overwhelming. Even though they were doing what he thought she wanted, she seemed sad about it, too. She said that she didn't like being left in their home by herself and they both wavered. For a moment their shared pain almost stopped them from doing what they knew needed to happen.

Fred tried to convince himself that the time apart would be good for them. However, he will always remember that day as a low point in his life.

He calls her each day now just to make sure she is doing okay and she always thanks him for checking in. She has started to see a counselor and asked if he would be willing to see the counselor with her sometime later. He said, "If it will make things better for you and for us, I am very willing."

Fred believes that his wife Jenny is a good person and he really misses seeing her. She said that she wanted this time to herself, so he is respecting that wish as best he can. Sometimes he just drives by their house though to make sure things look all right.

There is a feeling of numbness in Fred about the separate lives they have from each other. He wonders if that numbness is what Jenny has been talking about. She says, "You go away emotionally and you don't even know it."

He moved into a new condo downtown near the auditorium where the basketball team plays their home games. He enjoys being able to walk to the games and being close to the many people in the organization he has gotten to know over the years. Even the players are his friends. The young and friendly team members are a great crew of excellent athletes and human beings.

Fred eats at the local pub nearby and often shares a meal with his best friend John Dunlap, the play-by-play announcer. John has a great sense of humor and loves to talk basketball as much as Fred does. He knows Jenny and Fred have separated and he often asks how things are going. Fred says that he feels sad sometimes, but that he is hanging in there.

Soon after Fred and his wife separated, he began to blog because he had extra time on his hands and it gave him an opportunity to interact more directly with his readers. Writing for the paper is kind of a one-way deal. Fred writes the stories and the fans read them, but only rarely does he ever hear from someone who has read his work. With blogging it is different.

Fred's blog is called *Sports Heaven* and to him, this job <u>is</u> kind of a sports heaven. He writes the blog anonymously so that he can freely share his point of view. He gets responses to his blog every day and he enjoys *most* of them.

There are just some guys that have lots of opinions and don't appreciate anyone else's point of view. Fred thinks people miss out on a lot when they are blinded by their opinions. He wonders if having a closed mind doesn't get in the way of having healthy relationships.

The topics of *Sports Heaven* are usually about the players and the games. The regular season has recently started again and sports fever is alive and well. Fred often gets inside information and his readers seem to appreciate that, and the insights he shares.

Lately however, his interests have expanded beyond sports and he has been reading some books that are more about life. Fred decided that he has been too narrow in his life focus for a long time.

Fred's wife often said, "Can't you talk about anything other than sports?" He smiled and said he loves what he does and is just enthusiastic about the life he leads.

Jenny appreciates his love for what he does, but she admits to sometimes feeling jealous that his life fits his passion for sports so perfectly.

Anyway, Fred started to read other things and found that he is very interested in people and what makes them happy with their own lives.

Fred recently read a book about Michelangelo. He was an amazing human being and Fred thought that his passion for art and creativity was even stronger than his own was for sports and writing. He loved reading about him and learning about his incredible life. Michelangelo had so many challenges, but he just kept on going. Fred found his story to be truly inspirational.

Fred loved being inspired by the lives of those that live with such passion; that has always been one of his reasons to write about sports. He has found passionate and skilled athletes to be a true joy to watch.

One day Fred shared with his blog readers some of his impressions about the Michelangelo book. He was surprised to receive many positive comments from people who seemed to appreciate his passion for life. Of course, some comments were wisecracks about him becoming a philosopher or something.

Sports people seem to fall into two categories: the ones that have their own full lives and enjoy sports, and the ones for whom sports is their whole life and the rest of the way they live has no depth to it. Fred ignored the comments from those who were sarcastic in tone.

The supportive comments gave him courage to share more than sports in his blog and that opened up an expanded conversation that he enjoyed very much.

Actually, a few of his friends knew that he wrote this blog and they would come up to him and say, "Fred, I like the ideas that you share on your blog today. They got me thinking and getting me thinking feels good and important in some way." He wondered whether maybe others felt like that, too.

The blog began to be part sports and part questions about life — about what is most important. Fred found that he was becoming an explorer in search of more meaning in life. As he has gotten older and more thoughtful, he has opened up to bigger questions about what life is about.

His friend Robert, the team sports psychologist said that he's noticed that Fred seems happier lately. He thinks this new writing venture is just right for Fred at this time in his career and with the changes in his life. Fred smiles sometimes when he considers that he is changing and he enjoys the exploration.

Jenny even commented that his blog was turning into something that she was beginning to be interested in and Fred really felt good about that. He hopes that someday she will be open to them getting back together. Maybe this self-questioning is having more benefits than he had planned. He did notice feeling better about himself as he explored these new and meaningful questions.

Then one day something happened that would change Fred forever. He was sitting at his computer thinking about a book he was reading. Lately, he had been questioning who he was and the question seemed to come from deep inside. He found himself wondering "who am I?" and "where am I going with my life?" He then felt scared for a few minutes, because these questions seemed to make him uneasy.

Feeling uncertain, he then asked himself, "what really matters to me?" All of this got his interest stirred up. He wanted to explore more deeply what he intuitively knew inside. So he thought, "why don't I try an experiment and let my 'higher knowing' show me what the answers are to the questions I have through the use of my fingers on the keyboard?"

In essence, Fred kind of stepped back and let his inner wisdom be expressed. It was only a few minutes before his hands went to work. There on the computer screen were some very insightful ideas about who he was. He sat there in awe of the insights presented to him.

"What wisdom or knowing was in his heart but not in his head?" he asked himself. There was no immediate answer, but he figured if he kept on asking, the answers would start to flow. That is where things started to get really interesting.

It seemed that because he was asking or open to communicating with a knowing source, something happened. He felt this surge of power, like a flash of light and he knew in his heart that a direct contact had been made to some kind of universal knowing.

How that happened, Fred still has no idea today. But, there in that moment, he felt a God-like force take over his fingers and begin to communicate directly with him.

This initial contact was not part of his blog because it seemed too private and not for publication. That soon changed however, and today the world is still spinning from all "God" had to say. The "God" that spoke through Fred's writing was neither male nor female, but seemed a blend of both. He would later learn that "God" was unable to be categorized in many other ways also.

Now, I want to get on with the story about how Fred's *Sports Heaven* blog became known to millions as *The World According To GUS,* and how his life as a sportswriter changed forever. It is a damn good story. Please come along and find out what Fred's readers learned as "God" set the record straight.

PART 1

GUS Sets the Record Straight

*GUS - Who in the hell is GUS or should that be,
who in the heaven is GUS? We will get to
that part of the story very soon.*

CHAPTER 1

I remember the moment it happened as if it was just a few minutes ago. I was sitting in front of my laptop thinking about what I was going to write. All of a sudden a very strong urge came over me and the words started flowing. My thoughts were focused on how alive I felt all over my body as I wrote. Then I wondered why I was feeling so good.

Maybe this writing is something I am supposed to do, something about my purpose in life. I began to notice that if I let go, the writing flowed on its own. I watched as the words came across the screen and my mouth dropped almost to the ground.

"What the hell is going on here?" was what came out of my mouth.

The written words were, "Hi, Fred, I am God and I want you to do some writing for me. Fred, are you there?" God now became a voice I could hear.

It took me a couple of minutes to pull myself together and to respond. My fingers were ready but my heart was racing. I had visions of Linda Blair's head spinning and it scared me so much I couldn't stop shivering.

"Yes, God, I hear you. You want me to do what?" I said.

"Fred, I want you to write for me."

"Write for you? Okay, but why me?" I replied.

God answered, "I like who you are because you are just the kind of person I feel comfortable with and you are a genuine expression of one of my creations."

"I am what?"

"Fred, it doesn't really matter. Are you interested in the job?"

"Yes, I will do whatever you want"

God said, "I want you to help me. Are you willing to work with me on a project I have in mind?"

"Yes. How could I turn you down?"

"You can if you wish and I promise not to smite you. Just kidding, of course. I do not smite people nor am I the big scary guy in the sky that you should be shaking in your boots about. By the way, I did catch you shaking but that is not my preferred response in those I communicate with.

"I am kind of a laid-back creator/life force, if you will. I do not dictate how people should be. I let you all create your own lives. Is that not what free will is about?

"So, Fred, what do you think? Can we partner on this?"

"I feel so unworthy," was my response.

"Oh, stop that nonsense. You are one of my creations. How could you be anything less then worthy?"

"I guess you're right. Should I call you God?"

"How about Grand Exalted Ruler? I am joking. You have got to realize that I created the sense of humor so I have a pretty good one myself. So, Fred, are we on?"

"Yes, I will do my best to be of service to you because a part of me is very clear that this is what I should be doing."

"Stop *shoulding* on yourself! Will you do this with me and we can have some fun; share some ideas with your readers?"

"Yes, I will and I promise to do my best to have some fun and enjoy what happens."

"Excellent. My goal, with this project we are doing, is to set the record straight about who I Am and what my perspectives are on life, human beings, the planet and other tasty topics.

"I feel the record needs to be set straight because there are so many people on your planet, which you call Earth, who say they speak for me and they simply have no idea who I Am."

Fred queried, "I have a few questions. Why, God, are you writing through me? Should I change the name of my blog? Will I lose my job over this?"

"Fred, I understand your concerns, so let me address them. The truth is that I chose you because I want to talk to the men in the world. They might not come to God's Blog but they <u>will</u> check out *Sports Heaven*.

"With your help, I want my ideas to spread to everyone on the planet, not just men. But, frankly Fred, the men need the insights so badly these days. They just cannot seem to catch up with most women who are much better at living with their hearts as their guide."

"Yeah, I know what you mean. My wife, Jenny is so much better at listening to her heart than I am."

"Some men are good at hearing what their heart is trying to tell them. However, too often men really miss out on the higher knowing that comes from the heart. Instead, they live in their heads and block out or rationalize their feelings. So, Fred, I want to use your *Sports Heaven* blog. Can we create a special section and have my ideas posted there?"

"Yes, that's easy to do, I eagerly replied, what should we title it?"

"Whatever you want will work. Also, don't worry, you will not lose your job over this."

"I think I will call it *Thoughts On Life* and I'll tell people that if they check it out, they will get direct guidance from God. Oh, and thanks for reassuring me about my job. I love what I do."

"*Thoughts On Life* works great and it will evolve as we work this out together," said God.

"Wow, I am partnering with God on a writing project. Now, that sounds like a winning team, doesn't it?"

"Yes, it does, and thank you for being so willing."

God began, "Now, I want to get something straight with the sports readers right off the bat. I do not help teams win. I appreciate the prayers that are sent my way but, pray for your own life and the world, and stop this nonsense of praying for your team to win.

"Sports are just simple games and the need to win has gotten way out of hand. If anyone's peace of mind is based on their team winning, then it is time for them to rethink their life and get it focused on something that truly matters.

"That is not to put down what you do, Fred. You bring creativity and insight to your writing that benefits people. You express yourself in ways that are a credit to you and make me feel more hopeful about human beings.

"I want to be careful about not getting too preachy. I do not want to sound like one of those misguided TV evangelists. What they say is a disgrace to who I Am, plain and simple.

"Those poor misguided souls who follow them and give money are like sheep that somewhere along the way stopped thinking on their own and took the easier route of just following. I heard some human call them 'Sheeple' and sadly that fits too well. I did not create humans to be sheeple. I create sheep to be sheep and people to be people.

"Fred, you may need to keep me on track sometimes, because I have so much to say and I want to get it out there for people to read and think about as soon as I can. Also, you need to let me know when you need a break. As you might be able to already tell, I have so much I want to share. I get enthusiastic and I might go on too long."

Fred responded, "As a matter of fact, God, I could use a break right now. I need to get up and walk around and let this all sink in. I am still wrestling with my feelings of discomfort about finding myself writing for God. How can I deserve this incredible experience? There are many people more worthy of this kind of good fortune. I think I just need to feel more settled."

"All right, a break it is. But, first Fred, this self-doubt in you is not necessary. I have chosen to work through you not because of some idea of you being worthy, but because I just had a positive feeling that you and I might partner well on this project.

"This *not worthy* is old human garbage from generations of self-doubt. Let me help you break that cycle of doubt by letting those old thoughts go and instead we will work together in a way that will benefit many people. Is that a deal, Fred?"

"Yes, God, I would like to get past these limiting thoughts and serve you so you can make a difference. I do want to partner with you and will do my best to fully enjoy the moment instead of focusing on my doubts. Now, I'm going to go rest a bit."

As Fred lay down on a nearby couch, a whisper of peaceful energy filled the room and Fred was soon sound asleep enjoying his afternoon nap.

CHAPTER 2

God, in the form of a warm and comforting light, visited Fred while he slept. That light helped Fred feel open and reassured. When Fred woke up he remembered the dream visit and also felt uplifted because he now knew his life had taken on a much greater purpose.

He moved back to his computer, ready to return to work. As he did so, he settled into a calm and relaxed state knowing that his new friendship was real and things were going to get very interesting from now on.

"Hi, Fred. How was your rest?" God asked.

"Good, I feel refreshed and thanks for the visit in my dreams. It was very helpful."

"You are most welcome. Are you ready to go?"

"Yes, I am," said Fred.

"Your thank you reminds me of something I want to share with everyone.

"Fred, let's write this — I really appreciate it when people say thank you. As God, I get far more requests than communications of gratitude. I want to make this very clear, a thank you or thoughts of gratitude are very powerful prayers and very powerful creators of more things to be grateful for. Thank you is a magic phrase that has the power to create.

"I was thinking Fred, while you were napping, that I had some specific things I wanted to write about today, so let us add them to this message about being grateful."

"Okay, I am ready to add them whenever you are," Fred replied.

"The first thing is that I am a loving God. I did not create hell or a place of eternal damnation. Hell does not exist except in the minds of human beings. I want to make this very clear! **There is no such thing as eternal damnation.** That is fiction made up by the leaders of churches that want to make people afraid so they will be easier to control. All people are loved and forgiven even when they fall short of their divine heritage.

"I love all, unconditionally, as you love your children. There are no exceptions to that. **I love all people, of all beliefs, sexual orientations, and unique expressions.** I want that to be very clear. Can you put that in bold for me? Good.

"Love is the highest human expression and the best way to connect to me. Those that teach that I only love certain kinds of people are misguided and wrong.

"I want to repeat that I love everyone and I do not ever stop loving because of what you do or how you act. Please ignore any messages from churches that say God only loves you if you act *right*. That teaching is not one of mine and reflects a teaching from those lacking an open heart.

"As I said, love is the highest way for humans to be in the world. I appreciate so much the people who live to love, to give, to serve others, to be kind hearted and compassionate. I wish for everyone to love as much as they can every day.

"I think it is the New Thought people who say, 'What you put out comes back to you.' Yes, that fits with what has been defined as the golden rule and the Hindu idea of karma. The universal laws you find in all religions represent the closest understanding humans have about the higher truths.

"So, a reminder here — love is the highest law and those that love are living closest to my hopes for humankind. To withhold love in judgment of others is not my way nor should it be yours.

"I am on a roll here Fred, are you doing all right?"

"Yes, and I really appreciate all that you are saying." Fred answered.

"Thanks, Fred, I thought this would be something that you could get behind.

"Another issue I wanted to bring up is the idea of original sin. This idea of people being born in sin is nonsense. That again is the creation of human thinking that is totally false. There is no original sin. There is only the light and grace every human is born with. I do not create faulty creatures in my likeness.

"The only reason I can imagine that someone came up with this odd idea of original sin was to make people feel bad about themselves. People who feel bad about who they are can be much easier to control and manipulate. Think of religions as massive organizations trying to control their members and you can see them using manipulation to gain power over their so-called *believers*.

"Unfortunately, most of the religions created in my name have no idea who I Am. These religions have become giant corporations that seek to firmly rule their people and make up many ideas and rules for the sole purpose of keeping the people as powerless as possible. That is the opposite of my way.

"I always want to empower people. I have only created life that is a perfect reflection of who I Am. Sure, there are some that have lost their way, but they are still loved, and my hope is they will find their way back to me.

"Please ignore those who try to tell you there is something wrong with you. There is not anything wrong with who you are. Those teachings are a terrible mistake.

"I wonder if these so called, *believers* even want to hear the truth of what I have to say here. Time will tell about their openness.

"I have more to say about this but before I do, I want to ask you, Fred, what do you think about this idea that you are not born in sin and that there is nothing wrong with you?"

Fred thought for a moment before replying. "This is so enlightening to me. I was raised with 12 years of religious schooling and I got lots of lessons on how sinful I was and I felt pretty guilty. I think that is what chased me away from the church. I got tired of feeling guilty about being human."

"Yes, it is what drove you and many others away. It continues to drive people away because my creations are waking up more and more to a direct relationship with me. There is no place for guilt or sin in my world. They do not even exist. Those are mistaken human ideas full of limits and are totally disempowering.

"These false ideas I have been talking about were created by misfunctional people who had a personal agenda to gain power over others.

"Fred, what is that odd looking mark under that word?"

"It is called spell check and it says that word is misspelled. The right word would probably be "dysfunctional," Fred responded.

"So, I just made that word up?" said God.

"Yes, you did and I think you have the right to do that anytime you want."

"I love creating new words. Human languages are amazing but they do have their limits. By the way, I realize this is only in English and other people with other languages will want to share these insights. We will take care of that later.

"I was just thinking that I want people to know that the religions of the world are all doing the best they know how. Many of these organizations have massive components involved in monetary giving and compassionate action. They are on target with their work for those in need. When humans are giving, they are at their best.

"Here is another point I want to share. I think having money is a positive thing. I know that according to many churches, money is evil and yet they keep asking their members to give them more money for their *important* work. This is a clear example of the hypocrisy of their ideas. Having money allows you to live life more freely. Having money and investing it makes good sense.

"Investing in positive ventures works best for you and for the planet. Yes, I am an environmentalist. How could I not be? Earth is one of my most interesting creations.

"Having money means you can give more of it. Giving can make a positive difference when it is used to empower people and organizations — when it is used to help those in need.

"Recently it seems there has been a false dialogue going on about people in need. The idea of people in need being a problem in the world is the working of closed minds and hearts stuck in false rationalizations. Those in need are there to help you give.

"Giving that makes a difference is not giving to the symphony, opera or ballet, although they are worthy human expressions. This kind of giving is for your entertainment. Giving that matters is from the heart for those who truly need help, and for causes trying to make the world a better place for all.

"When people are serving the needs of others I feel joy. All your questions about giving can be answered simply — ask your heart what would be the kind and compassionate thing to do?

"Money is energy and the energy of greed and power taints the human view of money. Money that is used for food, shelter, education, health care, training and more, is money that is full of light and goodness. If you have lots of money, the more you share, the more your heart will sing.

"Fred, how are you doing? What is your reaction to what I have been saying?"

"I'm doing well. Thanks for checking in. Well, for me; I have at times struggled inside about making a good wage because I was taught that money makes people act greedy. My own experience is that people with money can be the nicest and most generous of people.

"So, I have had kind of an inner conflict about money. From your point of view, money is just the flow of energy, which can be used for a nice life and to enrich other people's lives."

"Yes, Fred that is right, money can enrich people's lives if they see it as energy in service of their needs and desires. Too much of what money is about is missed in the pursuit of some false idea of security. Real security is inside of you. When you have a sense of your higher nature and trust in that, the world seems a lot more secure."

"Security is a big issue in our world these days. I don't trust this emphasis on it by our government and how it uses the media to make us feel afraid of all these mysterious enemies," I replied.

"Fred, that distrust you feel is important to pay attention to because it comes from a place in you that senses manipulation. Your media appears to have become the information — spreading arm of those in power. It seems the investigative part of journalism has shrunk to a much lesser role.

"That brings me to the topic of fear. I think fear is, in most cases, unnecessary. Sure, when a train is speeding in your direction and your car stalls on the track, there is reason to be afraid. Too often though, fear is simply an emotional reaction to faulty thinking.

"Fear is living in contraction — guarded, protected and closed down. Fear is the opposite of love. I Am about love. Fear is the absence of connection to your higher self, to your expansive nature, and to me. Aligning with your heart, touching in with your spirit/soul and being mindful can neutralize fear.

"Fear is the major technique used by all power hungry governments, organizations and corporations to take power away from the people. As you noted, Fred, fear is being used in your country to control people. Throughout history, fear has been used by governments to convince people to give up their rights with the promise of being protected.

"My observation of human nature tells me that it is not the terrorist you should fear. It is your government and other power seeking organizations that are in fact the true danger. Look around you, do you really feel more threatened by terrorists or by your elected leaders and the decisions they make?

"Be very cautious about what you are told and what they want you to believe. I know, because I see all that is going on, and I am concerned that those in power do not have the higher wisdom to do what is right for the people. That brings me directly to several issues, but first I want to check in with you. Are you doing all right, Fred?"

"Yes, just great, your ideas really call into question what is going on. You will be seen by many as being very radical in your thinking."

"Well, I guess if questioning what is going on is radical, then that fits me. I gave everyone the ability to question things, but sometimes it seems that most prefer to follow the ideas of someone else and not question what needs to be questioned. I will comment more about the absolute importance of questioning as we go along.

"Now, on to another topic. Are we good to go, Fred?"

"Yes, I am running on lots of inspired energy today," Fred eagerly responded.

"Inspiration is such a positive force.

"There is no religion that even remotely understands who I Am. I have no religion. All religions attempt to define me, but get lost in false human ideas and the need to be right. That is not what religion is about. Many of your fellow humans are aligned with me when they say, 'I am not religious but spiritual'".

Fred quickly replied, "That's me, God."

"Yes, Fred, I understand why you and many others want to separate out religion from spirituality. Religions have become huge mega businesses and have lost much, if not all, of the spirit they came into existence to explore and share. I am deeply saddened by this development.

"I know places like the Vatican have a kind of perceived power in the world, but that is not real power. Real power comes from kindness and consciousness.

"True, the paintings in the Sistine Chapel are a magnificent human creation and a joy to see but they are not any more spiritual than a beautiful forest of fir trees.

"There are, as you can tell, many things that concern me about the nature of religion in today's world. One of my greatest concerns is the lack of women in the hierarchies of most religions. That is an example of male arrogance in need of control and reveals a great problem.

"Without the wisdom of the female heart, these religions tend to be dominated by old unquestioned beliefs. The old men that run these multinational organizations do so without much heart and without any real relationship with me or with what is spiritual. It is past time for that to change.

"I do not encourage anyone to participate in religious organizations that are not about truly exploring the spirit within. Avoid male dominated churches that are about people in power telling you what to think, believe, and feel. Many churches have lost their spark of spirit in the pursuit of worldly power.

"I will come back to that. Again, I don't want to sound like I am judging these religious organizations as bad. They simply have lost touch with their mission.

"I sent Saint Francis and many others to remind them of their priorities. Unfortunately, these organizations have a hard time leaving behind the power they have accumulated. Many churches have gone astray and replaced their spiritual mission with that of running a large, money generating organization.

"What is truly rich about churches is the community of dedicated people who want to connect to others. This seeking of connection is hopeful as long as those participating keep asking questions, truly seeking the truth and their own relationship with their higher nature. Living with an open heart and connecting to your spirit is the best way to live a meaningful life.

"There is one more thing I need to say because it is such a false teaching. The Catholic Church teaches that the pope is infallible when speaking on church doctrine. No man is infallible. That teaching is simply not true and should be questioned.

Look at the history of that church and it will show you clearly that there is no such thing as papal infallibility. The popes could have been a leading source of inspiration and light in the world, but too often, they have chosen old tired dogma over enlightenment. This is a sad use of leadership.

"Let us get back to this in another day or so. I need to let you do your job and I will be back soon," said God.

"Those were some challenging points of view, God. Many people could be upset by your words," asserted Fred.

"Yes, I know Fred. I never mean to upset people. My goal is to bring light to places where there needs to be higher wisdom."

"Thanks for sharing all of this with me and those that read this," answered Fred. "I am sure many will value it as I do."

"It is my joy to share it with a soul as open as you are and with all those who seek the truth.

"Oh, by the way Fred, it is time to ask your wife Jenny to go out to dinner. Let her know that you have much to talk to her about. If you are comfortable, share some of what you have been writing about for me. She wants so much to find a way to love you again. Her heart is open and she needs to connect with you at this deeper level you are exploring."

"Thanks, God, for your encouragement and ideas. I do want to find a way to bring us back together. I'll call her now."

That next night Jenny and Fred had dinner and they talked for hours. At times, she laughed like she used to when they were getting to know each other. She even complimented him on the stimulating conversation they shared.

"You know, Fred, if we could always talk like this, things would go well between us. I think there is hope because I can feel you in my heart again."

"Jenny, I feel you in my heart, too. I love you very much."

She gave him a kiss good night and said, "I hope we can get together again soon."

CHAPTER 3

A nother interesting development then happened in Fred's life. As he began to share these writings on his blog, many people wanted to interact with him via their comments. He explained a little about how he had come to talk with this wise voice he called, "God."

Fred said he wasn't initially comfortable using the name of "God" because it has been misused by so many who claimed they spoke for some god of their imagination. When he told the few friends who knew he was the author of the blog, they thought he was kidding when he told them he was talking with God.

One regular reader who often left comments said, "Sports is the way I fill space in my life when I can't seem to find anything meaningful. I have gone to a couple of churches in my neighborhood but they all seem so uninspiring. This section on your blog has got me thinking in new ways."

A friend of his named Will also sent him an email saying he really appreciated the ideas Fred was sharing. "I hope you keep on writing those ideas. They sure seem to be more alive than other stuff I read."

Fred sent him a message back saying, "Thanks for the note, Will. I'll gladly continue to write all that God shares through me."

Fred knew these guys didn't believe he was writing for God

but that was okay, because he also knew that someday they would understand.

His game coverage that night was fun as his team won their home opener. The fan spirit had really gotten energized again.

"Sports," he wrote, "not only entertains but can also lift us up. It inspires the viewer to get in touch with their own inner resources in areas in which they wish to excel. Athletes do amazing things with grace and determination. If they can, so can we."

Fred's readers saw him as a thoughtful writer who enriched them with his ideas. His writing had always gotten positive attention but lately more people found themselves uplifted by his words.

God reappeared on the third day. (Sounds like the Bible or something, but it was only Fred and God getting back together to do their work.)

"Hi, Fred, I am back and I have lots more to say."

"I'm ready, let it flow."

They both laughed and Fred's fingers readied for work.

"Before I get started," God said, "how did it go with Jenny the other night?"

"Thanks to you, it went really well," Fred replied.

"What do you mean *thanks to me,* I had nothing to do with it going well."

"Well, the ideas you have shared with me led to the most amazing interaction between the two of us. She even thanked me for the great conversation."

"I am so glad to hear that. You both deserve lots of love in your life. As a matter of fact, everyone does." And off God went, dancing through Fred's fingers.

"I want to again emphasize my most important thought for human beings — **loving is the best way to live.** Blocking your heart off to protect yourself is going against your higher nature and can only lead to numbness. Love is worth any risk you take.

"Speaking of love, I have regularly sent women with exceptional qualities to teach humans about love. There are always women on the planet who are recognized as embodying the qualities of the Divine Mother. There is one now called Ammachi who is one of my favorite lights in the world. Mother Theresa was one too. Women are naturally more in touch with their hearts because it is more acceptable for them to be so in most societies.

"India is a place where there are many women who are spiritual lights for the planet. India has a great soul tradition and I so much appreciate the love they bring to all they do. Many nations have women of spirit who are ready to teach about love and compassionate understanding.

"I do not ever encourage the withholding of love for any reason. People who withhold love cut themselves off from experiencing the world fully.

"I have an issue with the use of the word 'enemy'. The word enemy has been used to rationalize all kinds of terrible actions. There really is no such thing as an enemy unless you block your heart. Please know that when people are trying to get you to believe in an enemy, they are in search of a way to control you by cutting off your heart.

"That is never my way. We are all one family and there are no real enemies here, only closed hearts.

"I want to share some thoughts that are going to upset some people. Again, I want to say, my only intention is to shed light on things I feel have been represented incorrectly.

"Anybody who has issues with what I Am about to say is welcome to pose questions to me directly. When asking, be sure and take the time to stop and listen inward. I will respond.

"Human history is full of murder and wars in my name. None of those awful human acts, supposedly done in my name, had anything to do with God. They were all about power, ego and greed. I have never, ever supported people going to war and I never will. War is murder and is the opposite of what I teach.

"If you think people died for me in wars, you are wrong. They died for small-minded, greedy and power hungry men who have no idea who I Am. This history of misinformation about the intentions of leaders must be corrected. Wars are always wrong. There are always other solutions to be found before things get out of hand.

"Love is the highest expression of humankind and war is about as low as humans can go. Glorifying soldiers and other warriors is to glorify murder. Soldiers kill because they are programmed to ignore their higher values and the guidance of their heart. The idea of *duty* for the good of the country is false programming by ego dominated minds.

"I remove my name from any links to those acts of murder. War and killings are never, ever for me. I want people to be very clear about this. War in my name is a lie."

Fred spoke up and said, "That is going to upset a lot of people who have claimed God as their guide in what they do."

"Yes, it should upset them. It may hurt to be confronted with the lies humans tell each other about war and other rationalized ways they mistreat each other.

"While I am on the topic, in your country you have elected leaders who claim to be guided by me. This is nonsense made up in their minds. I do not align with any political point of view. Those that claim I do are making those ideas up to rationalize their own actions.

"Here's a good basic rule — never trust someone who claims

to speak for me. Find your own truth, listen inward and only be guided by what opens your heart and mind. If you are closed down, angry or judging of others, you are far from me.

"I encourage you to be skeptical of any teachings or writings claiming to be the word of God. Go inward and ask your heart and soul if they feel true to you. Always go towards what your heart and soul know is right. Your heart and soul are direct lines of communications with me.

"Politics and religion never mix. One is, in theory, about living by a higher truth and one is about seeking approval and trying to gain power. Politics, by its very nature, is complicated because of the dishonesty that goes with approval seeking. Those that attempt to mix these two fail at both.

"There are leaders who call themselves Christian in order to get your vote, but who never act in any ways that are compassionate or kind. They show no love and acceptance, they show no understanding of differences, they show no compassion for those in need, except maybe their own. This group is about power, not about me.

"This is all about their ego's needs and they should never be followed. I am surprised they have any followers. What has happened to the human mind that it gives up so much power by not questioning those that are obviously driven by power and greed?

"This is not to say there are no well-meaning leaders because there are. Those that lead from compassion, that encourage acceptance of all and seek to support personal understanding have things to say that are worth exploring.

"One of the reasons I decided I needed to speak up was to help clear the airwaves from the static of people speaking from ego and claiming to know me in order to spread their endless misinformation. These self-proclaimed ministers of God, in reality, have no idea who I Am or what my message is.

"The judgment that comes from people who are self-righteous should tell anyone who is paying attention that these people have no idea who God is. If compassion is lacking in any way, that should always be a warning to ignore their words. Those that lead without compassion are confused and are missing the key ingredient, the heart.

"I find myself getting energized as you write this, Fred, because so much has been said in my name that is a total misrepresentation of who I Am. I have come to set the record straight and these are some of the many issues I wanted to make very clear.

"To know me is a personal experience only. Being a member of a church whose ministers have often lost touch with their own souls out of greed and the pursuit of power is not the way to know God. The human ego has taken over many churches and has totally confused many who say they speak for me.

"No one speaks for me except me.

"**This writing is the first writing of my words ever in human history. My direct words have never ever been written before now.**

"If you quiet yourself and listen, you will feel the truth of my words. If you want to know the higher truths just ask, I will be there. That is all you need.

"Participation in spiritual communities can be a wonderful way to enrich your life. These communities however, must emphasize that everyone can have a personal relationship with God, and not give you their understandings as if they are the truth. Only you can know your own truth.

"Fred, this all seems intense, how are you handling it?"

"I'm doing well and so will most people who read this. I suspect it will just take some time to sort out this new understanding from the programming we have all received. I now understand that the only way to know what is truth and to know you is through one's own search. Everyone can explore their own ways of knowing and of finding their higher wisdom."

"Yes, Fred, you are right. I gave every human being an inner wisdom, a wise heart and a working brain to sort out his or her truth and an infinite soul in order to access all they need to know.

"There have been many great spiritual leaders on the planet, but they are almost certainly not the leaders of huge churches whose purpose is lost in the confusion of power and greed. Men (mostly) who want more and more power have always been scary in human history, because their way almost never worked out for the good of the people.

"Fred, I also want to write about the positive qualities of human nature. I feel the need to set the record straight about that, too."

"That would be an excellent idea because most of us have learned too many limiting ideas about ourselves," replied Fred.

"I agree, Fred. There is so much to appreciate about human nature. Humans have been given a magnificent brain to think with and an endless heart to love with.

"They have the ability to be creative and what they create is simply amazing. There is true genius in their music, painting, design, writing, scientific theories, technology, dance, and so much more. I so much appreciate the creative force that flows through the minds and hearts of human beings.

"I love to see the wonderful paintings of great artists and even just enjoy the brilliance of colors and images in the many styles of painting.

"I love to watch dancers as they fly through the air and turn music into a beautiful physical expression of movement.

"I so much enjoy the human voice as it soars through a wonderful song like Handel's Messiah, or an opera or even as it just rides a great beat.

"The designs of buildings and structures can be so eye catching and up lifting. Technology is ever expanding and impressive. Even a beautiful garden can so alter your sense of the world and the beauty of nature. There are truly exceptional creators and performers in the fields of education, drama, sciences, math and even athletics.

"So much of what humans have is worth admiring. You just have to walk around a city and take in all the human creations to see what comes from such vast and deep inner resources. Walk into a shopping center and look at the variety of things you can have. Go to a car dealer and purchase a vehicle with the latest in design and function. I can go on and on.

"Also, think about all the organizations that have been created to make the world a better place. People all over the planet have started their own programs for water conservation, world peace, river clean up, compassionate housing, food for the hungry, protection of wildlife, and thousands of other organizations are driven by their own sense of purpose and following their own truths. I Am very impressed when I see the human spirit on a mission to make a positive difference."

Fred answered, "Thanks God, for the reminder. I too, forget the huge range of creativity and genius we humans have. It seems as important to focus on what is working and what to appreciate, as it is to question that which needs to be questioned, doesn't it?"

"Yes, what you focus on does certainly color your experience of the world. Both appreciation and questioning are key elements in the evolution of the human species. An appreciation of what already **is,** motivates humans to stretch themselves. A questioning mind is one that stretches itself beyond any limits it may have.

"I want to also appreciate the ever-evolving sense of human understanding and consciousness. There are great traditions for exploring human understanding in many cultures. There are those people who can write lucidly about ideas and those that can tell real stories that move other people deeply. This takes special talent. There is so much to appreciate and I will say more as we go.

"Fred, let's take a break for an hour or more. What will you do? Is a nap in order?"

"Actually, I wanted to go for a run. It is a nice day and a welcome break from the rain that seems to bless this part of the country for months at a time. I find that keeping fit gives me lots of energy for life."

Playfully, God said, "Running, now that to me is the perfect exercise because all you have to do is put on some shorts, shoes and a shirt and you can go anywhere, for as long as you want. Do you mind if I ride along in your body to feel how it feels?"

"No God, not at all. I have never had a *passenger* but knowing you, I am sure it will enrich my experience."

They were gone for about 60 minutes and then after Fred's shower they met back at the computer.

CHAPTER 4

"O kay, God, I am ready to get back at it," said Fred enthusiastically.

"Thanks, Fred, for taking me along. Running is such fun in a body that likes to run and is strong and fit."

"Yes, it is my favorite thing to do and it serves me very well by keeping me healthy. I tell people that running shoes are the best health insurance you can buy."

"Fred, did you say health insurance? I appreciate that you have your own methods for healthcare. I could write a lot about insurance as a fear-based business that tries to make money from people's illnesses and insecurities, but I will restrain myself. If I had you write about every questionable business practice, we would never finish writing.

"Let me get back to setting the record straight about who I am and all the misinformation spread by people who claim they are speaking for me. I want to again clarify that **there is no one on planet Earth who speaks for me.**

"I only have *individual* relationships with my people on this planet. No religion or any church, pope, elder, priest, rabbi, imam or minister represents me. They all speak for themselves and I urge you to question everything they claim comes from me. It does not. I want to make that very clear. Only I speak for me, and only with each of you on an individual basis.

"This blog is written by me through Fred and I Am grateful for his help. This is my only attempt in the history of humankind to speak out to everyone.

"I have never really talked to individual humans much about how to view me. I am often called God in your world. There are TV ministers and many others who have used this name in such a way as to disgrace it. Please feel free to call me Spirit, Great Spirit, Source, Creator, Divine, Higher Power, or even God if you want.

"I Am always available to you by whatever name you call me. Although I have to admit to confusion about why you swear using my name. It seems an odd way to reach out to me.

"I Am the collective wisdom of the universe. I represent the most expansive mind, the fullest expression of love, and the highest consciousness. I Am not in human form but I can be if I choose. I Am neither male nor female. I Am the harmony of both. I Am not really in any type of physical form but I Am much more like a flow of energy, consciousness, love and light.

"To see the brightness of my light directly would be blinding. I Am kind and caring. I have infinite powers of creativity. I Am eternal and without limits.

"All the qualities in me are in you. You, as others on Earth have said, are a spiritual being having a human experience. You came from me as source and when you die you will rejoin me as source.

"God, I have an idea," said Fred.

"What is it, Fred?"

"I think the name God is very limiting because of all the false claims made in God's name. Can we talk about another way to address you?"

"What a good idea, Fred, do you have some recommendations?"

"Well, I thought we could put together a name by listing some of your qualities or some of the other ways to describe what you are. Then, together, we'd come up with a new name.

Fred continued, "I suggest that we use descriptive names like Presence, Universal Mind, Higher Guidance, Soul, Spirit, Source Energy, Great Spirit, and others."

They worked together for at least a half hour coming up with different words that all worked. Then, they talked about combining these words and finally, they began to experiment with the first letters of each word to see what they might spell out.

After awhile, they both began to laugh because a name did come about from playing with words and letters. That name was GUS.

It meant —

God, Guidance (Higher and Inner Guidance)

Universe, Universal Mind, Unity Consciousness

Source, Soul, Spirit

So GUS was created that day to describe the "Infinite Knowing Creative Force of the Universe". They chuckled and agreed it was better than "IKCFU".

Then they both had an idea for the title of the blog — *The World According To GUS*. They both agreed to wait awhile and see if this title was the one they really wanted. Before long, they decided that it was.

GUS was now free of all the human baggage and mistruths put on the name of God.

They both were joyous about this shift. Fred felt relieved from having to use the name "God", because it had so many negative connotations from his years of religious schooling.

GUS just smiled and said, "Fred, nice work. Now we can assist people to move into new ways of thinking, while leaving the past behind.

"Shall we get back at it, Fred?"

"I'm ready when you are, GUS."

GUS began, "There is in you the capacity to create anything you want or desire, if you allow yourself that ability. I gave you desire so that you would evolve in pursuit of the kind of life you want. With every stretch toward what you want, you gain more awareness. With awareness, comes the desire to stretch yourself even further, and this is the source of human evolution.

"Yes, I created the evolutionary process, but not the world in 6 days or whatever the story is. Nor do I know anybody named Noah or find validity in any of those people who call themselves Creationist.

"There are so many crazy ideas and beliefs invented by humans about who I am and my so-called 'rules'. The only rules in place are natural rules and the rest are all false human inventions.

"I want to get back to the subject of desire. Desire is a positive force for good. Any other ideas that say desire is wrong or causes suffering are inaccurate. The Buddhists have many wise teachings, but the cause of suffering is not desire. The Buddha was one of the most inspired human beings. His desire drove him to awaken.

"I created human beings, through an evolutionary process so I could experience all that they are capable of experiencing. Not as an experiment, but more as a way to further express my own nature. I Am always looking for ways to further express my divine nature for I too, am ever expanding.

"I suggest that expansion is the only reason you are here on Earth. You are here to fully express who you are, to realize your potential, to always be expanding and evolving.

"I love all my creations no matter what you do. Even the darkest, most unkind among you who hurt, hate and kill, I love without conditions. That does not mean I think these actions are right. To do harm is never right.

"Your own thoughts and feelings get in the way of you being a more direct reflection of all that I Am. I invite you to set yourself free by always opening your heart and mind. Then you can remain connected to me and together we can grow more deeply into all that we are.

"The human concept of the collective consciousness is true. I recommend you take quiet time to tune in to that knowing, for it fully represents the collective wisdom of the universe, which includes all that I Am.

"To say that you don't know or have access to me is incorrect. In the silence of your spirit, I linger in waiting to communicate with you.

"I encourage you to know me and the innate wisdom and capacities that are in you, as they are in me. Follow your heart's guidance for it is always a doorway to knowing that you and I are one.

"I want to make it very clear that what is waiting for you when you fully awaken to all that you are, is the liberating power and riches of the universe. What is mine is also yours.

"I am always available to you if you need to talk and especially if you are willing to listen. I will guide you directly if you want. Just come to me and talk to me. Tell me of your needs, ask me for guidance and I will gladly respond to you and help you have the life you desire.

"I trust fully in the innate goodness in every human being. In some, this goodness has been buried in abuse and pain, but it is still there, and I can help you reclaim it if only you ask and are open to receive.

"I hope all of this makes sense to you. Please excuse me if I have challenged your view of who I Am. It is my intention to do so, because most of what you have been told about who I Am is not correct.

"My hope is that each of you will explore your own sense of who I Am and what kind of relationship you want with me. Let the reflection of me *in you* come out fully into the world. Then, everyone's combined light will eliminate the darkness of those who have lost touch with their hearts.

"Hey Fred, how are you doing?"

"Wonderful! I am so inspired by your words and how great it is to have you working through me."

"I meant to ask, how are your readers responding to my messages?"

"The site hosting my blog called earlier and said they had to place the blog on a bigger server because of all the traffic coming to check out the "Thoughts" page."

"You mean the word is spreading?" asked GUS.

"Yes, it is, and there are many comments, most of which are very thankful for the validation they feel for being in alignment with what you are saying. I do get a number of comments that were very *unchristian like* from people who say they are Christians."

GUS responded, "I expected there would be quite a stir and it has started. Thankfully, the questions are beginning to flow as the truth hits the fan of delusion. Fred, do not fear these squawkers, many have loud voices but lack courage and when confronted with the truth, they will shrink away.

"Speaking of loud voices, I was thinking of talk/opinion radio. I find it very interesting that people in your country listen to the raving personalities on talk radio and actually pay attention to what they say. There are a few thoughtful voices out there but most have no idea what the truth is and just simply are making things up as they go.

"I am thinking of one of them who smokes cigars, has a history of drug problems and is run by a huge ego. This guy spreads nonsense, hate and fear. If you listen to him, stop — turn off the radio and listen to your own thoughts, the thoughts of those whom you care about, and even to me, if you wish. Those you love and I are a much better program to be tuned into.

"People who spread opinions that are judgmental and unkind are the opposite of what I had in mind. I suggest that you stop wasting your time listening to them and instead open your mind to let in the fresh air in and start thinking on your own. I hope I am clear about the importance of thinking and feeling on your own. There is no need to search for your truth through the minds of those who just like to hear themselves speak.

"You are so much more than those limited closed-minded opinions. The capacity in your mind is endless and you have the ability to see a much greater picture than the ones dominated by fear and control.

"I have more to say about fear but I will address that later. I suggest that in addition to turning off talk and opinion shows, you also stop watching nightly news. The habit of watching the news is detrimental to peace of mind. Most news is sensational and focused on fear to get your attention. If you stop watching it, life will feel better.

"Fred, how is it going? I didn't mean to put down sports news."

"No problem. When I look from a bigger perspective, I wonder about all the time and money spent on sports. I do enjoy what I do, though, and I really value what you say."

"There is no conflict there, just awareness, Fred. Awareness helps you make better and informed choices.

"How is Jenny?" GUS inquired.

"She is doing well and this weekend we are going to take a drive to the coast and if it feels right, we may spend the night at one of our favorite coastal hideaways."

"Nice plan, Fred. Are you all right with us going a little further today?"

"You bet I am."

"I want to say something about the other creatures that live here on the planet. First, I want to emphasize that all the animals, birds and other creatures I created, are here to share the planet with you and to enrich your life and theirs. They are not here to be dominated by humans.

"Killing them for sport is not what I had in mind. Killing them in general is not all right. Killing an animal to feed your family if they are in need, is a different story. Animal testing is not what I had in mind, either. The life of a lab animal is so sad and inhumane, and in no way fits with why I put them here on Earth.

"The people whose work is to care for animals and to keep them safe from human extinction work for me. "I love all my creations and that includes every one of them. I understand that sometimes humans wonder why I created mosquitoes, however."

Fred laughs and says, "In the movie *Oh God,* George Burns plays you and he says mosquitoes were one of his mistakes."

GUS laughs and says, "Well, I guess if George Burns said so, then I had better reassess those pesky little creatures.

"Those that say they kill animals to keep people safe are missing the point. These animals have the same rights to the planet as humans do. If an animal is a real danger then move it, if possible — don't kill it. If you are living in their natural habitat then you need to respect their rights too.

"To me, killing animals for their parts or as acts of greed is as awful as killing other human beings. What is it that makes killing an animal so appealing to some humans? Those that kill my beautiful creatures that you call elephants are heartless and they cause great sadness in me. Whales, dolphins and fish are also a part of my creation and are not meant to be killed for sport or profit. These beautiful creatures are so amazing and intelligent that to kill them is a violation of my higher law of love for all beings.

"I think of how much joy and wonder whales, dolphins, otters, sharks, tropical fish and my other creations have to offer, especially in the natural world. I wonder about the value of zoos and aquariums. Are they really necessary and how are they serving these creations?

"I can go on and on, can't I? I do think about so many things. I did give humans free will, but sometimes I question how they figure out what they decide to do.

"Place yourself in the shoes, fur, hides, flesh, skin of those you interact with, and ask how it would be to be them. If it wouldn't feel good or at least all right, then it probably isn't a great idea. Being thoughtful, compassionate, and taking other beings into consideration is always a good idea.

"There is so much you can know if you actually take the time to tune in and feel what the truth is. That is why I gave you that capacity, so you could see beyond yourself and live in a bigger world than just what you experience directly."

"See you later Fred" and GUS was gone.

CHAPTER 5

"Good Morning, GUS, I'm glad you returned."

"Were you concerned, Fred?"

"Yes, I was. It has been a few days and I was thinking how much I am enjoying our time together."

"Remember, Fred, all you have to do is find the quiet place in you and I will respond."

"Of course, I forgot, I must admit that I must have some doubt that it can be that easy."

"Today after I am finished, take some time to find your inner stillness and see how easy it is to make contact with me," suggested GUS.

"I will do that," promised Fred.

"How was the trip to the beach with Jenny?"

"It went so well. We had a wonderful time and we were intimate again and we both really opened up to each other. I feel so much better having my heart open again to her. It makes me feel like I love everyone."

"Yes, an open heart is such a wonderful thing isn't it, Fred? When you love someone freely and openly, you feel open to everyone, don't you? That is the way all humans are meant to be — open hearted and loving to each other. This kind of loving is so expansive and so full of caring and compassion.

"Intimacy is different than the more universal kind of love. Intimacy is about the connection two souls and bodies have and the potential for self-realization in that togetherness.

"Most humans have not even gotten close to expressing all the ways love can be explored and shared. You have a term called unconditional love. That is genuine love from me to you that can then be extended to others. There is no limit to how much of that love you can give. You can actually love yourself, everyone and everything else and have plenty left over to love your partner.

"I really want humans to come to realize that their capacity to love is without limits and can extend across the whole universe. Universal love, sounds like a great component of universal health care doesn't it?

"Love is the greatest healer, the greatest resolver of human difficulties. Oops, there I go making up a word again. I see 'resolver' underlined in red."

"The readers will understand what it means," Fred said.

"You are right, Fred. I appreciate the calm wisdom I sense from you lately. You are rising to the occasion of our task together."

"I am humbled by your appreciation and this opportunity to be so close. My heart is open."

"Thank you for your love. I want to say more about love. As I was saying before I interrupted myself, love heals, resolves problems, inspires, opens people up, creates wonderful relationships, expands compassion, caring, and so much more.

"All problems in the world have love as the solution. There is no human conflict that cannot be resolved through love, compassion, caring and empathy.

"I want to say that again. Every human difficulty can find a solution through love. This includes any problems between groups, between countries, between belief systems. There is never the need for war if love is applied as the solution.

"Yes, I am a pacifist advocating love as the path to a better world. My people during the 60's had it so right when they spread the message of peace and love. World leaders need to live by that idea now. The people leading your country and others need to find their hearts again. All problems can be resolved by love, understanding and compassion.

"Terrorism is wiped out by love. Terrorists disappear if they have understanding, compassion and love. They cannot fight against love."

"Thank you, GUS, for reminding us of the simple solution of love and understanding. Our country seems to want to complicate the issues and not focus on finding solutions that will work. Most ways to resolve problems are really rather simple but our egos get in the way. I guess ego uses fear as you suggested the other day to enhance its own power over others."

"That is right, Fred. All through history, ego-driven leadership in search of control has tried to keep the people afraid. That is happening in your country and many others even today. If the people feel afraid, they will give up their power to the government in hope of security.

"It is always a mistake to give up individual power and freedom to any government because they will take advantage of people who do so. Opposition to governmental policies is easily repressed when a nation is afraid.

"Ego driven people in power are not necessarily evil, just confused and arrogant enough to think they are right and should have all the power they want. Arrogance is one of the greatest faults of my precious humans. Behind arrogance is a closed heart and fear.

"If you are run by the arrogance of your ego mind it will cause major problems in your life. All wars come from human arrogance. I hope that is clear. Does it make sense that I would actually encourage an arrogant leader to start a war?"

"No," Fred said.

"You are right. I would never do that. I want to repeat something I said earlier. I have never ever encouraged any human being to go to war. Wars are preventable long before they happen. Hitler and other misguided leaders would never have gotten into power if love had been the highest law.

"Humans have gotten off track, closed their hearts, and then the worst kind of world becomes possible.

"Oh, by the way, I love even the worst of the worst. These wounded ones have lost their own hearts and that is a very sad thing. I will however, always welcome them back into their hearts.

"I keep coming back to love because it is the greatest of human capacities. I have come to share my ideas so all of you that are reading my words can find your way back to the full expression of your heart. Love as much as you can, all day, every day and the world will transform itself into the paradise it was meant to be."

"Thank you GUS, for all that inspiration. This is going to stir up lots of thoughts in my friends. I am so glad to be reminded about the power of love. Please keep on reminding us of the power of love so we never forget."

"I will, Fred. Let us take a break. What do you plan on doing?"

"Lately, I have found myself reading about and wanting to explore meditation so I can spend more time in the inner stillness you talk about." said Fred.

"Yes, that is an excellent idea. Meditation is one of the highest human inventions ever. There are many good meditation practices. I have explored them all, and have blessed those who also explore them, with insight, inspiration and inner peace. Meditation and prayer are so much alike, especially if prayer includes listening for my guidance. Prayer that is just asking without listening doesn't work. Meditation is a great way to listen inward and you can find me in this practice."

"Yes, so if I meditate, I can feel you inside of me." responded Fred.

"That is a good way to express it, Fred. Because in the silence, the *you* that feels separate can dissolve away. In silence, you can reconnect to me and to the collective consciousness of all. I would encourage all humans to practice meditation. Meditation is an effective way to get past our lesser nature and open to the greater fact that you and I are *one*. We are *one* in every aspect of our being. If you take the time to really do a full exploration of who you are, you will find your nature is divine like mine. In fact you are in complete unity with me at all times.

"I like the image of each rain drop, as it falls into the ocean, becoming the entire ocean. You are both the drop and the entire ocean. I Am the ocean of consciousness and you are always part of me.

"I want to state that in another way. Now imagine that you are connected to everything on your planet. Then, imagine that in addition to your connection to all on Earth, you are also one with all in the universe. The entire universe is within you.

"Imagine everything in the universe being inside of you. This all-inclusive view is accurate. You are not the center of the universe. The universe is what you are made of.

"You are so much more than you realize. Everything is part of you. That is why love is so important. You must open to loving all parts of you. You must love the terrorist in you, the wounded human being in you, the mad leader in you, the deranged killer in you and then all will come into balance and harmony.

"I know that for many that seems too simple. That is the fault of their not questioning their own limiting thoughts. It is all amazingly simple. Love is the way. Love is my way."

"Fred, I was going to take a break, but I just got inspired and off I went. I hope you are not too worn out?"

"No, I am good and feel energized."

"Good, then let us break now, and I will be back later."

CHAPTER 6
_____

Later turned out to be the next day. But that was no problem for Fred, because in the early evening he had quieted himself down and opened to his own stillness. There he thanked GUS for all the support and for allowing him to be part of this incredible writing experience. And he sat quietly awaiting a response.

His wait was short.

"You are welcome, Fred. I will be back around midday. I hope that works for you."

"It does. I look forward to spending the time with you and to continuing our enlightening writing experience."

"Me, too."

They then conversed about some private matters about which Fred sought his guidance. An hour later Fred just sat in silence vibrating with the insights and energy he had received in his session with his writing companion.

Then Fred went off to cover the evening basketball game. When he arrived at the game there were a few of his friends who stopped him in the hallway and spoke in amazement at what they had been reading in the new section of his blog.

"So, you weren't kidding, were you, about God having you write for him." said one friend.

"No, I wasn't kidding, I am having the most amazing experience." Fred smiled.

They had lots of questions for him, including how God came to now be known as GUS. He patiently answered each one as best he could. He always arrived early for his game coverage, so he still had plenty of time for dinner after they had all gone.

The news was out and his blog was now drawing attention all over the planet. One thing about the Web is that information can travel very fast and this kind of unique happening had the web buzzing.

Fred had kept his own name off his blog and so far his friends had kept him a secret. He knew that it would only be a matter of time before someone found out he was the writer. Reporters can be very resourceful, as he well knew.

The game went well. His team won another early season contest and he wrote his article for the next day's paper.

His wife called after the game and said how much she was being affected by what GUS was saying. She then asked, "Is it really okay to call God, GUS?"

Fred said, "Yes, GUS is the name they had agreed upon and he told her more about the discussion."

Then she asked, "When can I see you again?"

"How about tomorrow night for dinner?"

"Okay, but I am making it for us," she said.

"What time should I come over?"

"I will be home after five so any time after that."

"Can I bring something?"

"Yes, how about a nice bottle of white wine."

"I'll be glad to. And Jenny, I am really looking forward to spending the evening with you."

"I am, too, Fred. I'll see you after five."

The next day GUS was there when he said he would be and as always he checked in with Fred.

"How is the fame going?" GUS asked.

"Well, of course you know, people are all of a sudden much more interested in my blog "Thoughts" section than in the main section on sports. So far they don't know my name, but that is bound to change soon."

"I know. Are you all right with that?"

"I'm feeling good because I know that it will all work out," replied Fred.

"I am glad you feel that way."

"Are you ready to get back to work?"

"Yes, I am.

"Yesterday I talked about the other creatures on the planet and how humans need to act with kindness and compassion. Today I want to talk about the planet.

"I created Earth and to me, it is one of my most beautiful creations ever. It was given to humans as a gift when they had evolved enough to be aware of it. I assigned humans the job of taking good care of it and for centuries they lived in harmony, but that changed when things went industrial.

"Now the planet is a mess of human made pollutants. There has been a shift going on from a healthy planet to one which is on the way to becoming nearly uninhabitable. I am very concerned about the lack of care for the planet.

"I want to make a very clear statement about the way I would like humans to better take care of their home. I suspect it will not surprise you that I hope people will treat the Earth as a loving partner. This loving partnership is very necessary or Earth will become a place that is no longer friendly to human habitation. This beautiful globe and all its wonderful creatures deserve the best of human care.

"Yes, I Am sure some will call me another one of those tree

huggers. They will be right. I love and hug all my creations. Tree huggers and I share a great respect for the planet.

Those that use and abuse Earth cannot be allowed to continue. It is harming the future for all living beings. The choice is this — make taking care of the planet a priority or ultimately the planet must take care of itself. That may mean clearing away the damaging forces. Yes, Earth is in trouble as your scientists have said. I am encouraging you to fix things before it is too late. That *too late* is much closer than you think."

Fred asked, "How come people ignore what is going on?"

"I am concerned because my people have gotten so over-whelmed by what they are trying to pay for and the stresses they deal with in life, that they have lost touch with what is really going on around them and on the planet.

"The human struggle for survival puts paying attention to the health of the country and the globe more in the background of their thinking. This has to change at many levels. I do not think this is the way it should be.

"There is plenty to go around and lots of human genius, but fear is dominating the dialogue for change. I am writing to tell everyone to do their best to overcome letting fear run their life. Fear is a powerful human reaction, but it isn't reality.

"If you watch the nightly news you might think fear is what you should feel. I want to make it very clear that fear is not your natural state and that any fear you feel is generated by unexamined thoughts.

"When fear is present in you, acknowledge it, and then open your heart and focus on love, what you feel grateful for, and on what you want to create in your life. There is much to love, much to be grateful for, and much to be explored and created in your life.

"Fear will drop away if you are focused on the positive results you want to create. Open your heart and just love yourself, those you care about, your destination in life, and what you want to make happen. Stop letting fear run you. Always, in any way you can, replace fear with positive anticipation, joy, gratitude and love.

"You have endless possibilities wired into who you are. I know because I oversaw the wiring job. I suggest taking it easy and simplifying things so you have more time to love and to be."

"Sounds like many people are lost," commented Fred.

"Fred, you are right about that. So many have lost touch with why they are here in this life. Humans are here to love, to be joyous and to express themselves as fully as they can.

"A lot of people have gotten overly focused on doing and having more and they don't take the time to listen inwardly in order to find out what is most important. Life is so easy to get caught up in. You get too busy and then you go, go, go until you drop. That is all right once in awhile when you are on a mission to do something extraordinary, but as a way of life, it is too much doing and not enough of just being you, in a relaxed and enjoyable way.

"Life is full of choices, take the time to explore what choices will create the life you want and what ones just keep you going down the same old tired groove. You are the sole creator of all your experiences while living in the world.

"I am going to say that again just to make sure you hear and feel this. **You** create your experience of the world. That means you have the power to create your life the way you want it to be. I will guide you if you want. First, get clear about what you want and I will help you get there.

"That is all I want to say about these topics for now, but,

I am sure I will have more to say later. Fred, are you ready to change gears?"

"Yes, where would you like to go next?"

"How about a bike ride along the river?" inquired GUS.

"You know, I just got a new bike and I have wanted to take that ride now for days. Would you like to ride along?"

"Yes, I thought I might like to ride with you and experience a nice sunny day while riding a bike. I never have had that experience and now I can through you. I am looking forward to finding out how it will feel."

"I'll go change, then we can go down to the garage, get out the new bike and you can climb on board, or however you share my experiences."

"Yes, I will ride along inside of your experience. I wanted to talk with you about some things anyway."

"That sounds good to me."

Off they went and several hours later they returned.

CHAPTER 7

"That was so nice. I enjoyed the ride with you. The bicycle is such a wonderful invention. Riding along quietly and taking in the world at a speed that is just right for seeing all there is to see. Thank you, Fred."

"You're welcome, GUS. Thanks so much for your words of encouragement. I am deeply touched by your kindness towards me. I am so glad to have you as my friend and as my guide."

"My pleasure."

"Let's get at it, Fred."

"Okay, let it roll."

"Today, I am going to stir the pot a lot more. I have much to say about this topic and I want you to know that it is very important that you understand what I am saying. Fred would you please ask questions if something isn't clear to you, because I want everyone to understand what I am about to say."

"Yes, I will ask if I am unclear at all about what you are having me write for you."

"All right, let's begin. The story of Jesus is a story from the Bible. He did exist in the form of one of my sons coming to earth. Just like every one of you do. You are all my sons and daughters. Jesus was no more special than you. The way in which he was different than most people was that he more fully realized his own divine nature.

"You have all the same possibilities to do miracles that Jesus had. You simply have not realized those possibilities in yourselves. Please, do your best to understand this as clearly as you can.

"You, as my human creation, have all the abilities that any other human being has ever had on this planet. There is Jesus in you, Buddha, Mary, Mohammed, Lao Tzu, Gandhi, the Divine Mother and all other great human beings in history are in you.

"Jesus was famous for his teachings about love but most people who teach about his ideas seem to ignore those teachings on love or place them in some minor role. His teachings on love came through me, as he was in direct communications with me all of his life.

"Those that say they teach what Jesus taught usually have only a guess as to what they are talking about, since there is little in the way of an accurate accounting of his life. I know this because I watched Jesus with love as I watch you all.

"His ideas which came from me, have mostly gotten lost through the inaccuracies of men who created their own stories. Too many of the teachings of Jesus have been misunderstood by well meaning human beings with little self-awareness or consciousness.

"Jesus was well ahead of his time and most did not understand the depth of his loving message. As I do, Jesus taught about love, compassion and understanding for all humans and all beings. He did not select those that should be loved. He did not condemn, he did not judge, he did not make everyone who was different than him wrong.

"The Bible is a wonderful storybook full of lessons, but it is not the word of God. I know that goes in direct contradiction to what many have been taught. The Bible is the word of men, basically only men who have put together a story that they thought people would benefit from hearing. The Bible cannot be the word of God because it was written by men who mostly had no contact with me at all.

"Many of those today that call it the word of God also have no relationship with me. If they did, they would know it is not made up of my words. The history of the Bible is full of inaccuracies and it is simply a storybook that has been used by many as a book of authority. It has no divine authority.

"Let me again make this point very clear. The Bible is not the word of God. It is the word of men, many well intended, but few with actually any kind of direct relationship with me. This is a collection of stories, many of which originate before the time of Jesus, yet claim to be part of his life. I know this flies in the face of all that many have said and heard for the last few centuries.

"This is another reason that I came. You must know the truth. The truth is that the only way to know me is through your direct relationship with me. No church or religion can do that for you.

"The reason that the Bible is used as my word is because those who claim so, do not know me and use this collection of stories to validate whatever kind of human agenda they have going on in their heads.

"As I said before, I do not have anything to do with the TV ministers or any of their claims. All of this is a kind of group confusion and I suggest you wake up from that confusion and find your own truth. No one, that means not **anybody** else, can tell you your truth. You must find it your own way. Stop giving up your own search for truth by letting others tell you what you should believe. *No one* knows your truths but you.

"I don't mean to be harsh, in any way, sharing this. I want you to know that you all can know me in your own quiet way. My request to you is to follow your own heart and spirit and stop following others. They can only misguide you and too often they have no sense of their own truth. You are loved and that is the most important thing to realize. You can only know me through your heart, your listening, and your eternal link to me — your spirit/soul.

"There are good and well-intended ministers, monks, rabbis and priests out there. They are the ones that are humble and full of heart. These good men and women, you can talk with and get guidance from, but ultimately it is you that must discover your own truths.

"Those that know me are not run by their ever self-glorifying egos. They are kind, loving and accepting of all people and all beliefs. There is no right belief system; beliefs are just thoughts and these thoughts should be questioned to see whether they have some value to you or not.

"Groups of other truth seekers can also be helpful. Together you can explore ideas and practices and encourage insight and awareness. Expanding your consciousness is what enriches your life. The more conscious you are, the more open you are to knowing me and to realizing your higher nature.

"There are also on the planet now, some excellent spiritual teachers that have ideas worth contemplating. They can help you explore but they can't take you to me. You are the only one capable of finding me for yourself.

"The Buddhists don't have a God in their belief system but they tap on my door regularly in their silence. They are all about listening inward.

"To join me doesn't mean you have to identify me as God or GUS or by any other name. You could experience me as energy, light, a knowing, stillness, as the divine in all things, your higher self or whatever feels like something beyond your ego, body, personality, feelings and thoughts.

"I Am beyond the ordinary but simple in my ways. I Am peaceful and understanding. I can be direct and gentle. Try me out; explore how we can communicate easily with each other.

"I want to again remind you that the Bible is a collection of stories that can be helpful, but they are stories. Anyone who claims the Bible is the word of God/GUS is wrong. People who want you to live by what the Bible says are totally misguiding you and are probably very misguided themselves.

"I am repeating this because I want to be as clear as possible to all those who read what I am saying. So, one more time — the Holy Bible is not holy but has been made falsely holy by those who do not know me. It is a collection of stories from long before the myth they called Jesus ever was on the planet and many of the stories were written long after he was gone. The book has no authority.

"Fred, I think these ideas today are really going to upset some people and I wish it wasn't so. The unfortunate part of this is that many people have been misled for many generations. I want the misleading to stop so I am letting everyone who cares to, read what I have to say, see from the place of a deeper truth, see from my eyes."

Fred says, "I am not worried about the reactions because what you say makes so much sense to me. I am however, not a minister who has spent all of his or her life preaching from the Bible as if it was the word of God."

"Many were doing what they thought was right, but they had no relationship with me to guide them to the truth. I want them to come to me now and ask how they can continue their work and do it with the real source as their guide.

"There are so many churches and religions claiming their authority under the guidance of the Bible. These organizations are all based on false teachings and on even more false inter-pretations. I suggest they reorganize and become human service agencies and use their resources to feed and care for the people. No churches ever need to be built again. There are many more churches than are needed already.

"Yes, without question, some of the churches vibrate with the energy of so many prayers. These buildings are made much more sacred by my people who have brought their concerns, requests and questions in prayer than by the churches that own them.

"Some of these churches are so-called famous halls of worship but worship has nothing to do with me. I do not want worship-ping human beings. I want conscious and loving human beings.

"There is so much more to real truth than the words spoken down at you from the pulpit. These are not ever my words; they are the words of humans trying to get you to act in certain ways.

"I hope after you read and think about what I Am saying, that you turn from the religious righteousness and instead search inwardly for the wiser teaching of your heart and access me directly when you need to get back on track.

"One other note about the big churches and the TV minis-ters — stop giving them money. They are not about me and the money is not for me. I do not ask for money. I Am the creator of all things, how could I need money?

"They want the money for themselves and whatever programs they may have, which are often not from the kind of higher place you would want to support. I suggest you wake up fully and quit following these people, for they are not the way to me.

"Another key point, which I have mentioned before; there is no hell. There never has been nor will there ever be, except what you create in your own life. If you create a painful and disappointing life for yourself by your choices and unwillingness to grow, then you may create your own hell on Earth. That hell is not my creation. I only create out of love.

"There is no heaven. There never was nor will there ever be a heaven. You can make your life here on Earth quite heavenly by the choices you make. If you are loving, kind, joyous, understanding, open-minded and willing to explore and express who you are as fully as you are able, then life can be a heaven on Earth.

"I will share some good news later about what happens after this life on Earth.

"Fred, I am ready to bring this writing to an end today."

"I'm also ready to call it a day," replied Fred. "I think people will be really stirred up and I am sure they have enough to think about."

"Yes, I am sure they do also. I am concerned that this Bible thumping, I think humans call it, has gone on way too long. It seems to even have gotten more intense over the last ten to fifteen years. I really wanted to set the record straight about this."

"Well, GUS, I think the record is straight now as far as anyone who reads this goes."

"Yes, Fred I don't think I have left much of a doubt."

"How will others find out about these ideas?"

"Well, I chose the internet because it will spread the ideas quickly once people know they are available," said GUS.

"I will want this series of blogs turned into a book when I am finished. The book will be low cost and free to those who can't pay. It will be available to all who really want to seek the truth of who I Am and how they can relate to me."

"That book will be a bestseller," responded Fred.

"Yes, it will and I hope all lives will be enriched by what I have to say."

"Yes, GUS, they will be."

"Let's go back at this in a couple of days. I want the dust to settle some before I stir it up again. I will check in with you each day and you can let me know when the time is right to go forward with setting the record straight.

"Be in the light of love, Fred."

"Thank you for your blessings, my dear friend."

"You are welcome," GUS replied.

Later that night, Fred and Jenny had dinner at her home and again their talk lasted late and Fred stayed the night in the bed they had shared for many years. It felt good to be home.

The next day they talked about Fred returning home and they decided to take it slow and easy, so that when they did come back together it would be not only with an open heart, but also with the consciousness necessary to keeping on growing together.

CHAPTER 8

F red was at his keyboard just finishing one of his sports
columns when GUS arrived.

"Hi, Fred, how are you doing today?"

"I'm doing well. I did think a lot about what you have been
talking about lately. I have received a flood of comments on the
blog, and frankly, some of them are scary and they are from
ministers and people that say they speak for God. There are
some really mean spirited messages with no part of love at all
in what they have to say.

"Heresy is the word that comes up often and someone said
I should be struck dead. There were many bible verses directed
at me. Fortunately, I think I have remained anonymous."

"Sorry, Fred, for the barrage, I would gladly take those comments and address them in the blog if I thought there was a
willingness to be open to the truth. I will keep on addressing
the issues that need to be and leave it up to the higher self in
each person to sort it out.

"Your friends who know that you are the blogger are keeping
your identity safe. I very much appreciate that."

"Yes, I called those that do know and told them the shit is
hitting the fan and I need them to keep me safe. Each one agreed.
There are six very close friends including Jenny who know I

am the author of the blog. I feel confident they will keep me anonymous.

"I feel as though my safety could be in danger if my name got out there. There are radical people who like to eliminate those who think differently."

"That is part of the history of humankind. The world has lost leaders like Lincoln, Gandhi, Martin Luther King, and too many others because their viewpoints were in opposition to what some people thought was right. I will keep you safe but be aware when you are out in the world," replied GUS.

"I will and I trust fully in you watching over me," said Fred.

"This is a perfect place for me to go on with my thoughts that I want to share. How did humans decide it was all right to kill off those who thought differently or acted differently then they did?

"I think of the natives of your land, who were killed en masse because they were simply in the way. Such murder has been going on for centuries and is against all that is right and loving.

"Opposition is essential to a healthy democracy. In your country, Fred, more and more opposition is pushed out of view. It seems people who stand up against those in power are quieted down rather quickly these days. I see more and more power regulating all aspect of society. This is very dangerous for your country's future and is a big global issue.

"The spying that is going on is an epidemic and run by the paranoia of the ego-mind. The original checks and balances seem to have broken down.

"I have to say again that fear is used by those in power to keep all others under their control. Fear is a powerful weapon against the masses if you want to manipulate them.

"I know I may sound like some conspiracy theorist or something, but, as GUS, I see many things that I think most citizens should be deeply concerned about. That is another reason why I am taking the time to share my concerns.

"As I have said before, the mix of religion and politics is dangerous. As an objective observer, I have the capacity to view all that is going on without judgment. It is always my hope that the right choices will be made to protect the freedom of human beings for all future generations. Any group of churches that join together to be a political force has truly lost its focus. If they were genuinely religious in their nature then they would not be part of party politics. Politics is about governing and about representation.

"Religion is not part of that, but the men who run religions have let their egos take over and are trying to force their religious views on their fellow citizens. That is totally and completely wrong. Religions should not be recruiting organizations. Religions are not here to save anyone. Sadly, they have become much more about taking care of their resources than taking care of the souls and needs of the people.

"I have watched so much being said in the name of religion that is supposed to be about God, but has nothing to do with God. I feel sad that this has happened and I will continue to speak up about how religious institutions have gone wrong.

"I want to make this very clear, I have no religion; GOD/GUS HAS NO RELIGION.

Anything that is stated to the contrary is wrong. I Am not the member of any religion nor is any religion really about me. They all claim to be about me but if they were, they would have to disband because they would see that a true spiritual life is about the individual's relationship with me. I Am not the God of any particular religion nor am I associated with any kind of church.

I Am where there is silence and love between my people and me.

"There are many giant organizations called religions but they are only rarely about the spiritual life and about living with compassion. I know I have shared similar ideas before, but I want to repeat myself because I see it as so important.

"These mega-churches are only about organizational power and influence. Those in the higher structures of organizations like religions serve their purposes first, but not really those of the members. Religion is big business, and that is all it is. That may sound too harsh but it is the reality I see from my vantage point.

"If you are a member of a religion, I suggest you resign from it and find your own truths. If you do so, you will feel much better because you and I will be in contact directly. There are some churches that are inspirational and uplifting because they do spread compassion and higher human understanding. If there is heart, consciousness and wisdom, then you can get real benefit.

"Coming directly to me is always best whether you are in a spiritual community or not.

"I am a loving GUS as I have told you very clearly throughout these writings. I do not question to upset you but instead to inform your choices about life.

"There are many who want you to believe that their beliefs are *the truth*. You have the free will to believe them. Many others have graced this planet with much wisdom and compassion, but they have never tried to recruit you to believe as they do. These would be better teachings to explore.

"I have been deeply touched by the kindness and insights of many of your fellow human beings. The light of insight is a beautiful happening. I get to watch that happen all over the globe in the silence of people coming into their own highest self-realizations.

"You too, have been given the ability to expand your self-awareness, to be filled with the light of insight, to live in union with me, and to know and live in love and joy.

"That is everyone's nature. You have been given all these gifts and they are yours to explore and to live. Any group or gathering that encourages and supports the full realization of these gifts is worth being part of for it represents the highest of human knowing. Those who gather to do such work, gather with my light shining there in support.

"I have this idea that organizations that provide free support and encouragement to those seeking spiritual growth and realization could be in every community. This would make it much easier for citizens to live and act consciously. Consciousness groups based on living in awareness and guided by higher wisdom would make for an enlightened planetary citizenry. That has real potential to me.

"If you want to start your own group of spiritual support, I will guide you to help each person realize their potential. These gatherings for conscious living can be a positive force for transformative change.

"I want to mention one type of person who claims they are doing what they do in order to be closer to me. Those that practice self-punishment or extreme forms of personal denial need to explore a more compassionate way of treating themselves. To do that in my name shows a very confused state of mind. To be unkind to yourself, to put yourself down, to berate yourself, serves no positive purpose. Please be loving to yourself if you really want to be close to me."

"Fred, how are you doing? I guess it is break time again."

"I am doing really well, GUS. I think the conscious living support groups are a great idea. There are many people hungry for support for their inner journey. These groups could serve people all over the world like AA serves those in recovery. There could be meetings someplace every night to support their own growth and awakening."

"I agree Fred, about the longing in people. People of all ages seem to get to a point where they long for more meaning. If churches transitioned from social control organizations to places of spiritual encouragement, then people who seek conscious support can find it in places where it could have been all along.

"These centers can become the place where enlightenment is explored and truth is discovered. Of course this journey of discovery begins on an inner level that most likely takes place in your own home.

"I put out these ideas with the hope of people taking them and using them for the benefit of all. There is so much that can be done that will enrich everyone's lives."

"I plan to get a group of my friends together who are open to living more consciously and have you guide us to a higher expression of ourselves, said Fred.

"Excellent. I will bring all the light you will need. Let us take a break and I will be back soon."

CHAPTER 9

"Are you ready to get back at it, Freddy, old boy?"
"Yes, I am at your joyous service, GUS, old infinite one."
They both laughed.

"Speaking of old, what is your age GUS?"

Still laughing, GUS said, "Well, I have been around since the beginning and will be here forever, I guess that makes me really old, doesn't it?"

They both laughed for a few more minutes.

Fred said, "I love our time together."

"Thank you for being such a genuinely nice human being.

"By the way and not meaning to get serious when we are laughing, but old is a linear time thing and a human misperception of reality. You are more like energy going out in multiple directions many of which you are not even aware of. You do not get old, but are ever renewing"

"I guess this means we are back to work, GUS?" asked Fred.

"Yes, it does.

"It is time I speak of what is possible in the expression of the highest human nature. There has been a continual exploration of wisdom from the spiritual cultures of India, China, Japan, Tibet, the Middle East and the western contemplatives. This exploration has uplifted human understanding.

"The divine within every human being is infinite and expansive and waiting to be realized. This means you have an endless potential to be explored and expressed. The challenge is to continually keep opening your mind and heart to allow the further expression of your highest nature.

"This energy potential within you takes time to harness or your socks would be constantly blown off, your hair would stand on end, your eyes would be squinting from the light, and your body vibrating at a level that would shake the earth on its axis. Do you get the picture? Like a power station that takes the power and steps it down, you, too, are mostly unconsciously self-regulating the energy so that you can handle it.

"I want you to imagine you are growing to the full realization of these inner resources. Imagine that you can manifest what you want. You can.

"Imagine that you can heal whatever ails you. You can.

"Imagine a life filled with love, joy, and meaningful expression. You can make it happen.

"There is all that you would consider miraculous within you.

"There is the source of the sun and the universe as your operating system.

"There is all the abundance and richness of the planet inside of you waiting to be expressed.

"There is infinite and endless potential residing in you that would take many lifetimes to even begin to explore.

"There is a heart that is big enough to love everyone and everything on this planet and is, in fact, big enough to love everything across this galaxy and all galaxies.

"There has never, ever been found a limit to the creativity that is inside of you.

"The brainpower in you is bigger than the biggest computer

and still much of the mind's potential is untapped.

GUS chuckled and said, "I get so excited about human capacities that I start sounding like a seminar leader trying to inspire the best in my audience. That sounds like what I am up to, doesn't it?

"I want the best for each human being on the planet. There is plenty of what everyone needs here on earth, so that every human being can have the life they want.

"Even if, for now, too much of the financial resources are in too few hands, there is still what is needed. You can have whatever you want in this world of abundance.

"Now, I want to take this discussion towards questioning the money issues that are so prevalent.

"Fred, how are you doing? Can I go on?"

Fred eagerly replied, "I'm very interested in what you have to say because from what I see, greed is the dominating force in the world."

"Your perspective, Fred, is very accurate. Frankly, I'm greatly disappointed in how the pursuit of more money and profits has become such a negative force for the well being of both the people and the planet. The rich keep getting richer. The money schemers manipulate the outcomes and the wealthiest keep inventing more ways to create more for themselves.

"Everyone could easily have as much as they need and want if people's greed wasn't attempting to control everything.

"I invite those that have so much, to be very generous and use their resources to make a positive difference. The more they open their hearts and give away, the better they will feel. It's wonderful to live to give and to enjoy what you have.

"I know the whole money thing will stir those that have and those that do not. Poverty, despite what many churches have advocated as virtuous, is not better in my eyes than being rich. Money is just money.

"Poverty is not what is meant for my creations. I meant for everyone to live a prosperous life. Those who let money be their only goal, and have it dominate their lives, have lost peace of mind and contact with their hearts.

"Those that preach that poverty is a good thing are usually not poor. Those that want you to believe that less is better cannot be trusted to look after you. Humans live in a rich world and having what you want is how it is supposed to be.

"The accumulation of things will not bring happiness. There are many who try to convince you that the right car, house, partner, or shoes will make your life happy. They are not interested in your happiness, only in selling you their products or ideas.

"Churches that ask for money by trying to convince you that it is good for your soul, or you will be forgiven, or it will be easier to get into heaven are best ignored. Don't give money to any organization or individual that uses fear, guilt, righteousness or arrogance to get you to give."

"You know, Fred, I am very capable of ranting about things, am I not? I see that. I get to experience all kinds of new things about myself through this desire of mine to set the record straight.

I Am growing and expanding as each of you does in your lives. Please know that if I say things multiple times, they are important to me and are worth your time to think about.

"I want to talk about something else again because I feel it is a very important issue. Human arrogance generated by what humans call the ego-mind is a huge problem on the planet. Arrogance drives very bad decision-making. Arrogance is the result of an ego gone out of control.

"People and governments that think they are above the law

are arrogant. People that feel superior to others are arrogant. People who think they know what is good for others are arrogant. People that think they have the right to control others are arrogant. People that ignore the good advice of others because they want to be right are arrogant. People who are dishonest and cheat to get ahead are arrogant enough to think whatever they do is all right. People who say I guide them, yet never have sat quietly enough to listen to what I have to say are arrogant."

"How do arrogant people get into such positions of power?" asked Fred.

"Fred, they gain power because people confuse their arrogance with confidence. There are many human problems caused by people being so easily fooled; problems such as wars, lack of healthcare, corporate dominance, intolerance, dysfunctional government, poor leadership and more. Conscious, questioning people are not so easily fooled. "I have a lot to say today, Fred. Am I boring you or tiring you out?"

"Neither, but I have to chuckle sometime because you are going to make a number of people very upset with these words. They are going to want to attack you and prove they are right."

"Yes, my friend, I am sure many are more interested in being right than knowing the truth. Their responses will be the same rationalized responses that have led to all the destructive things perpetrated by their ego-minds.

"That is enough about arrogance. It is a pretty boring topic.

"What is much more interesting to me is people and their many good qualities. I love that you can feel as well as think. You have an inner guidance system called emotions that can always tell you how you are doing.

"If things feel right, you know you are heading in the right direction. If you don't feel all right then you have to reconsider what is going on. The head is pretty good at fooling you but feelings always tell the truth or at least lead you to it.

"Feelings are great indicators. Once you understand your feeling responses, you can use them to guide your life.

"The emotions that should never be ignored are the reoccurring ones that are trying to guide you to a better and more enjoyable life. Taking the time to at least acknowledge your feelings keeps the messages coming to guide your life."

Fred and GUS decided they both wanted a brief break. Fred got up and walked outside to get some fresh air. His mind felt energized and his body wanted to move. He also sensed that GUS wanted to go back at it soon.

"All right, Fred, are you ready?"

"Yes, I am at your service because working with you like this is so enlightening for me."

"Fred, I, too, benefit from such close contact with a human being. I feel enriched also. But as you can sense, there is a hot topic I want to talk about, said GUS.

"Yes, you seem abuzz."

"I am, because I realize I have very strong feelings about what I am about to say."

"Feelings?" observed Fred. "This is my first awareness of you stating You have feelings all though your energetic responses indicate You are full of feelings."

"Fred, you are so observant. What I can say about your observation is that I tend to be pretty even keel about my emotions. This setting the record straight has unsettled that evenness and I frankly feel that is a very positive thing for me.

"Without others to interact with, my existence tends to hum along without disruption. Coming here to share ideas has disrupted that hum, which seems to me to be a positive development."

"I love that you can grow, too," reflected Fred. "As you have said, each of us is continually expanding and that includes you. What is it that you feel so much passion about?" Fred asked.

GUS replied, "I have something that I need to set the record straight on. I call it the ultimate human guilt trip.

"I have been thinking about this for quite some time and it is time to clarify once and for all this false human idea. The ultimate human guilt trip is the cross.

"The cross is used to symbolize the sacrifice of Christ. Christ did not die for your sins. If he was crucified for anything, it was because of ignorance and prejudice. It was not because all humans need to be saved. That is simply not true.

"There was never a need to die for anyone's sins. It is when arrogant leaders start wars, that millions die because of the sins of their ignorance.

"The cross represents the Churches' idea that you are saved. That is a totally false idea. If you like to wear a cross because it looks nice, that is all right, but do not think it has anything to do with me.

"How could such a horrible death have anything to do with what I would want? Would I truly have created all humans as innately sinful and in need of salvation?

"That is totally false and nothing to do with who I Am or what humans are about.

"The next time you see a cross, please forgive all those who have used it falsely in my name. I do not attempt to guilt people into following a belief system of such limited ideas.

"The churches with the big cross over the altar or on the top of their buildings are just missing the point. I Am about love, not pain and suffering, not ignorance and prejudice, not sin. I hope that is now cleared up for all those who seek the truth.

"I may be saying too much for people to take in here because it contradicts another of the many false ideas that people accept.

"Am I alienating all my readers, Fred?"

"I trust not. Once they see you are merely inviting them to a richer and more direct way of interacting with them, free of guilt and sin, they will welcome that," replied Fred.

"I feel you are right, Fred. Should I go on then or should we break for awhile?"

"I am ready for a break."

"Break it is," agreed GUS.

Fred left to spend the evening with Jenny and didn't check back in until the morning. He and Jenny felt like their love had been rediscovered. Jenny was again full of joy and her heart was so open and understanding.

All those who had known the two of them were very happy to see them find their way back to love. This inspired their friends to help find their ways back to love with their partners.

CHAPTER 10

They reconvened the next morning, meeting at the computer for further dialogue.

"Fred, I am so happy to feel all the love that is filling your life."

"Me, too, and thanks for making that possible."

"I only invited a spark in you to re-ignite and for you to return to your natural state."

"Only?" mused Fred.

"I am cheering you on. Marriages and relationships offer many challenges for most humans. An increasingly small number of relationships seem to go very well and most struggle at least some of the time. Marriage is a human invention, not one of mine. In these times, marriage does not seem to have served a positive purpose for many.

"People who marry do so by their choice. Marriage is not something I encourage people to enter into. I do wish the best for them, but I do not bless marriages. They are already as sacred as the commitment they make to each other. This commitment is not for me, it is for them to support and encourage the fullest expression in each other.

"This whole shaming that goes on and people feeling bad about marriages that don't work out, is about humans, not about me. I do not think failed commitments are wrong. They are simply commitments that didn't work out or they no longer serve the individuals. The churches have misrepresented my views on this. I am sorry they do that because it really can mess up the positive possibilities of a committed relationship.

"Here is more to contemplate. I totally support the use of birth control so there are no unwanted children in the world. To be intimate only in order to have children is a perversion of the church. That is not my way. I gave humans the ability to make love for the pleasure of being alive and loving. I accept and encourage the full expressions of humans loving each other.

"What I observe is that those that rant and are filled with judgments about sex, often times are full of mixed emotions and desires themselves. It doesn't surprise me that some get caught in situations where they are acting directly the opposite of what they profess.

"I would encourage caution around those who go on about things that are sinful or not the ways of God. I suggest they would best be ignored because they are mixed up and not seeing clearly.

"Sex is normal, and not a sin; neither is thinking about it, dreaming about it or talking to others about it. Relax and enjoy this human gift and ignore all those who say it is wrong. They are the ones who are wrong.

"Having children is a wonderful thing, but children do best when they come into the world by choice. Preventing unwanted pregnancies should be part of everyone's education including a thorough explanation of all methods of birth control. That is a sensible and wise approach so that all children that are born will be loved.

"Those that oppose birth control because of so called religious beliefs have no idea what they are talking about and should be completely ignored.

"Abortion is up to the couple that created that beginning to human life. Ultimately it is the woman's choice. No laws should be made to limit that choice. Those that judge are following made up human beliefs, not any ideas of mine.

"What happens is always between the individual and me. No church, religion, minister or priest has the right to pass judgment on any of my children. Every person's purpose, including those who claim to work for me, is about learning to be a more loving human being, not to be more critical and judging of others.

"I hope I have made myself clear on these topics. Of course, you have a choice to believe and act in any way you choose. I fully and completely support the right of individual choice and I am always available for guidance along the way.

"Making your own choices is part of being free. You were born free of sin, karma or any other pre-existing limitation. You came into your life a mix of all humanity and totally free to become anyone you wish to be. You were created free so that you could choose and create the life you desire. You have all the inner resources to create this ideal life. You have the freedom to be fully you.

"The realization of all you are, will keep you busy all of your life. You are never finished exploring and expressing yourself. This *always expanding you* is how all life was created on the planet. Every living thing is always moving toward a more expanded expression.

"You evolve because you follow your freedom to fully express yourself. The more you live your desires and go for the life you want, the more you evolve in the light of new understandings.

With these new insights you seek to further express yourself and the evolution continues. All life is expanding in this way.

"Hey Fred, are we good to go further now?"

"Yes, we are." Fred replied.

"Good, I want to continue sharing my perspective. This time I want to talk about preaching. What an odd way to communicate with people. As a preacher, you stand above your people and lecture them about things you think I want them to know. Where did this idea come from and why does it continue to happen in churches all over the planet?

"Why do people put up with being told how to act or be? Sure, there have been greater speakers, more like wise teachers that have been worth listening to, but these are the exception.

"Preachers are too often very unenlightened people who think they have a higher wisdom than those listening. From what I can tell, it appears their goal is to straighten people out. This is nonsense and why would anyone waste their time being bored, scolded, or yelled at by someone who is probably more confused than they are? People who think they are obliged to listen to the self-righteous have always bewildered me. My hope is that people will believe in themselves enough to know their own truths and to follow them.

"Churches serve humanity if they take people higher, if they lift people up and show them the possibilities within them. That is a church at its best — a loving source of support that encourages the highest expression in each person whom they serve.

"Churches that are full of what you do wrong, the sins you commit and how lost your soul is, serve no positive purpose. Why would anyone in their right mind put up with that? I guess the answer is that they are not in their right mind.

"A right mind is where you believe in yourself, in your potential, in the divine seed in you waiting to blossom. A right mind is a mind that is open to the wisdom of the heart and importance of self-loving.

"This kind of mind is supportive and encouraging, not critical. This kind of mind is full of ideas and inspiration. A healthy mind is joyous, compassionate and fully accepting of you as you are.

This is the kind of mind that does not need others to set them straight or to fill them with rules and laws they claim came from me. All those rules and laws are from men not me.

"All human laws need to be questioned. It is wise to do so. The highest law of love and compassion needs to be part of every consideration or else that law is invalid in my eyes.

"I am not trying to start a massive questioning of all laws here, although that is not a bad idea. My point here is to remind those interested in the truth to question all those that say they have all the answers for how you should live. They do not and cannot have the rules for your life. You are your own rule maker. You regulate yourself.

"Governments spend too much energy regulating the wrong things while money driven organizations do great harm and go unregulated. All governments should be focused on what is good for the people and the planet.

"It is time to wake up and see the truth of what is going on in the world. Stop giving away your authority to others. Stop accepting *the party line* or the misinformation sent out by the corporate owned media.

"Yes, I Am a social critic because so much falls short of what humans are capable of. Ask questions, get to the root of the situations, and nose around until your gut/heart/soul tells you what the truth is.

"That is more than enough on the topic for now. I think I was guilty of standing on high and preaching at people just then. Fred, are you ready to take some time off?"

Fred responded, "Your points were stated with a lot of emphasis. To tell you the truth, I am ready to get up and move. I thought I would take a walk to the gym and go for a swim in the new pool. Want to join me?"

"Sure, the pool sounds especially fun. Isn't that where kids go crazy running around, shouting and having so much fun?"

"Yes, it is, but adults don't run around screaming and having lots of fun."

"Why not?" queried GUS.

"Good question, maybe you could start a new trend by having me run around screaming and laughing. You know where I would end up don't you?" asked Fred.

"I suspect it would be at the local mental health center."

"Yes. I'd be on a 24-hour hold for my own good."

"All right, I will act properly on our outing," promised GUS.

"Thank you for being so kind," countered Fred.

They were gone for several hours.

CHAPTER 11

L ater on, when they were back and refreshed, Fred and GUS
talked for a few minutes.

"Moving through water was a very unique experience for me,
Fred. Sure, I have all the oceans within me but I have never felt
direct contact with it like I did through your swimming. Water
is such a wonderful and beautiful creation, is it not? That may
sound like I am blowing my own horn, but in fact it is me being
in amazement at the wonder of creation. This planet is truly a
gem of limitless worth."

"Yes, GUS, I love the idea of the ocean having a whole other
world within and it is just out there and a mystery to me as I
stand on the shore looking out."

"Yes, it is full of mystery. Let us go to the beach one day,
Fred. I think I would like to go for a walk out into the ocean
and meet my underwater world directly. Of course, I could go
there on my own. But I have a feeling you, Jenny and I will be
there before long."

"That sounds like a fun trip."

"It will be, Fred. Shall we get back to work?"

"I'm ready," responded Fred.

"I want to talk about kindness. I love kindness. I love those
who are kind to themselves and those who are kind to others.

Kindness is one of the simplest and purest forms of love. Kindness is acting from the place of an open heart. If you listen inward I will always show you ways to be kind in every interaction you have. Kindness means treating others with them in mind. Every day provides a chance to spread kindness.

"If you want to know what will make you feel happy and help bring peace of mind, the answer is to spread kindness everywhere you go. When others are depressed, down or struggling, be kind to them. Kindness will help open their heart again.

"Kindness is a healing force that soothes even the most damaged souls. Acts of kindness can help you find real joy. Kindness makes you want to give more. All kind acts come back to you in wonderful ways.

"The opposite of kindness is not caring. Not caring comes from not paying attention to what is going on in the world around you because every human being has the ability to care.

"Those that have lost the ability to care have been very wounded, often by their upbringing. All people are born caring. To lose your caring heart means your heart has missed out on being cared for.

The most uncared for people in your country end up on the street, in treatment or in prisons. Living on the street is not necessary in a civilized world. There are plenty of resources and all can be fed and have a place to sleep at night. I hope people can wake up to this idea and make sure all humans are cared for in compassionate and kind ways.

"Now, I want to address the prison system in your country. Why are so many in prisons? How have we failed so many that they have ended up incarcerated?

"Prison is only of value as a temporary place for containment for those that have lost their way. Very damaged people may need lots of structure but prisons do not provide the needed treatment. Most people in prison shouldn't be there because it is not helping them or society. People do not heal and or get better in prison. They lose more of their humanity and they are less able to return to live a life that contributes. Prisons are a faulty solution to societies' problems.

"Executing people is not the answer. Violent people ended up that way because most likely they have been violated, neglected and are in pain. Killing these sad and wounded people lacks true humanity and does nothing to get to the root of society's issues. As Gandhi, a wise human being said, 'An eye for an eye will make the whole world blind.'

"It is my suggestion that prisons be eliminated except to house the most violent of people. Then all others can be worked with in ways that will allow them to become positive members of their communities again. All executions should be stopped.

"I want to also say a few words about forgiveness. I want to remind everyone of this option when dealing with things that have gone wrong. Forgiving others for their wrongdoing is the act of an open heart. Forgiveness shows that you have chosen to let your heart win out over pride. That decision I applaud.

"Forgiveness is so much more powerful than choosing to remain upset or angry. Forgiveness is actually more for your benefit then the one you forgive. Forgiveness allows you to move on and free yourself of the baggage of the past. Forgiving is letting go of that which needs to be released. This allows you the freedom to live with more joy and love in your life.

"The most important forgiving you need to do is of yourself. If I can forgive you, then you can too. Forgiving yourself drops the unnecessary self-judgment and allows you to be all right with yourself. If I believe in you and your potential, so can you.

"Forgiveness is one of the ways to release yourself from the emotions of the past. Why would you settle for holding yourself back when you can decide to set yourself free?

"Fred, how are you doing?"

"I am doing okay, but I could use a break. I want to go have lunch with Jenny. Would you like to join us?"

"Yes, I would. I would enjoy meeting Jenny in person, although I won't be in person," laughed GUS.

"I know what you are saying," replied Fred. I very much appreciate your words about forgiveness. I need to let go of my old feelings about my parents. They were just doing the best they could."

"Yes", said GUS, "they were, even if they hurt you by not showing they cared. They simply did not know how to do that."

"I am beginning to understand. I see how I have carried their emotional withholding in my own life with the way I have been with Jenny. It has almost felt more natural to withhold than it does to let my heart be giving. I feel protective of my heart; afraid of it being hurt," admitted Fred.

"Yes, Fred, that fear of an open heart was passed on by your parents. It is time to let go of that unexpressed tangle of emotions. Finding a way to love them even though they are gone will allow you to more easily keep your heart open to Jenny."

"Thank you for the ongoing insight you are providing for me. I feel like a sponge soaking in all that you share."

"Are you ready for lunch, Fred?"

"Yes, I am. I'll just give Jenny a quick call to let her know we will have a guest."

They left a few minutes later.

CHAPTER 12

The lunch was fun. With some practice, Jenny learned to relax with the unusual guest speaking through her husband. (GUS chose to speak through Fred as a way not to scare the people at the nearby tables who otherwise would have heard a disembodied voice.)

She got to ask him questions and share her thoughts. The three of them talked for several hours longer after they left the diner and headed for a long walk along the river, over one bridge and back across another. Portland is a city built on a river and the downtown is filled with all kinds of bridges.

There were many things discussed and lots of laughter shared by all three.

"GUS," Jenny said, "I have never thought of you as having a sense of humor. How odd that we humans see you in such limited ways. I suspect there is so much more about you that we will yet discover."

"Jenny, you are so right about the limits people have put on who they think I Am. I Am not human but I have all the human abilities and a number of qualities humans have yet to discover.

"I wanted to communicate with people directly because I wanted them to understand that I feel all that you feel. I have compassion for all that you struggle with. I know what you go through and I can laugh just like you. I do love to laugh. This lunch has been so wonderful because I got to know another exceptional human being."

"Thank you, GUS, for being so kind in your words," said Jenny.

"You are welcome, Jenny. You know Fred loves you very much."

She looked at Fred and said," Yes, I know he does. He and I will be okay now that you have helped us both find our hearts again."

"I give you my blessings and fill your life with the light of a loving relationship with me."

"I am very grateful to have my Freddy back and for the grace you send our way."

"My pleasure," replied GUS.

Jenny left to return to her work. When she arrived all her employees asked her where she had been because she was beaming with life and happiness.

"I have been with Fred and a special friend of his," explained Jenny.

"Who was the friend and what did he do?" said one of her oldest and closest friends and working partner. "You look so full of life."

"This friend blessed us with such wisdom and joy."

"Blessed you? You talk about him like he is God or something."

Jenny smiled and went into her office and everyone just stood there for a few minutes in wonder at what was going on with this person they all loved.

Back at Fred's house, GUS said, "Jenny is such a kind soul and the two of you is what I had in mind when I thought of people joining together in love."

"Thank you. She is a true joy to me and a real gift in my life."

"Are you ready to get back to it? I have more ideas to set the record straight about."

"Okay, I'm ready."

"I feel it is important to address the male dominance of most religions. Any religion without women as priests or ministers and as leaders is out of balance. There cannot be truth with only one sex represented. Male dominated churches often lack heart. Women need to be an integral part of any church structure. Women tend to balance out the male need to be in power and to dominate. Women more often bring heart, compassion, feelings and understanding. Men have all these qualities but often they are under realized or dominated by the ego's needs.

"Churches and religions that only allow women to be in passive roles are not to be trusted. This means women are seen as *less than* and that is wrong. I would encourage people to stop attending those male dominated churches because they are so out of balance and out of touch with me. They cannot be of any real use to anyone.

"The kind of male arrogance that I have mentioned already is a major problem in most religions. The need to control and dominate means they are run by ego and have no contact at all with me. Be wary of anyone who wants to be in control and put people in roles that are secondary to their authority. That is dangerous and not in the spirit of what I had in mind.

"Women are sacred beings with sensitivities that enrich the quality of the human race. Please remember that all my creatures are to be treated with respect and love. There are no lesser humans, there are no lesser animals, and there are no lesser beings for they all are made up of who I Am."

"Jenny would so much appreciate your words and so would the wonderful women that work with her," interjected Fred, "the force of those women working together as advocates for equal justice is recognized throughout the region where they advocate for many important causes."

"I know she is doing good things in the world and I am sure it is with great force," agreed GUS.

"Yes, she is and I am so proud of her. Hey, I need to stop for now. I have a game tonight to cover and a friend to meet for dinner."

"Sounds like it is time to call it a day."

"Yes, my thought, too." said Fred.

"I will be back in the morning. What time works for you, Fred?"

"How about 10? I will be up late putting tonight's article to bed. If you want to join me and experience the game from a writer and fan's point of view, you are welcome to."

"I know where to find you and I just may," responded GUS. "Until later…. Enjoy!"

Later that night at the game, Fred had a very uneasy feeling that he was being watched. It wasn't GUS because that energy was always so comforting to be around. At half time Fred noticed that a menacing looking guy was following him.

As he sat back down at the reporters' table after half time, he felt even more uneasy. He closed his eyes and asked for GUS to watch over him and all those there at the game.

Soon there was a big disturbance under the tunnel where the players had just passed on their way to the court. The police had surrounded two guys that looked very suspicious. There was a commotion and then there was a shot fired. One police officer went down and all the rest jumped on the one with the gun and his partner.

After a twenty-minute extension of the halftime, the crowd

was told there had been a disturbance and two people were arrested and taken away. Fred thought he had heard a shout about "God getting back at you," as the gunman looked Fred's way.

No one saw what Fred saw. The gun was aimed at him but the officer moved in as soon as he saw it being drawn.

GUS said to him in that moment, "I am here to watch after you. It appears things are getting out of hand. I knew the reaction would be strong but you have been discovered in some way. We need to rethink this and make sure you are safe."

"What about Jenny?" worried Fred.

"Yes, I was thinking about Jenny's safety, too. Are you all right Fred? Go on back to your game and we will talk tomorrow. I will make sure you and Jenny are all right."

"Thank you," answered Fred.

There wasn't much that could distract Fred from his work and he was soon fully focused on the game. He did notice that the hot dog he'd had at halftime was not settling very well in his stomach.

CHAPTER 13

The next morning two plain-clothed police officers were knocking at Fred's door just after 9 am. He was just getting out of the shower when the doorbell rang. He yelled, "I'll be right with you," and soon he was standing at the door in his shorts and t-shirt with his hair still wet.

"Can I help you?" he said.

"Yes. Are you Fred Jacobs?"

"Yes, I am and who are you?"

"I am Detective Cooper and this is Detective Stewart." They showed their badges.

"How can I help the two of you?"

"Can we come in? We have some questions to ask."

"Oh sure, come right in and have a seat," offered Fred.

"Can you give me a few minutes to get clothes on and can I get the two of you anything?"

"Yes, take your time and no, we don't need anything."

A few minutes later Fred reappeared and handed each of them a cup of coffee.

"Thanks, Mr. Jacobs," said Detective Cooper.

"Mr. Jacobs, Chief Parker says hello."

"Tell him hello from me," answered Fred.

"We will."

"Mr. Jacobs, did you see the disturbance at the game last night?"

"Yes, I did," Fred said, wondering where this was going.

"Well, one of our guys was shot and we guess he got a bullet meant for you."

"Why do you think that?"

"Do you write a sports blog called *Sports Heaven*?"

"Yes, I do but I keep it anonymous."

"Well, someone has found out."

"Why would they shoot at me?"

"As far as we can figure, you've been writing some stuff that has upset some people."

Cooper continued, "I read through your 'Thoughts Section' and found myself confused. Did you write all this stuff and why are you doing that? Who is this GUS?"

"Actually, this is a bit hard to explain, but I am just a sports writer and one day I heard this voice. God, who we now call GUS, came to me and asked if I would write for him and help set the record straight.

"He said he had become concerned that there were too many people claiming they were speaking for God and they were not. GUS decided it was time to let everyone know what God thought."

"So you are saying this voice has taken over your writing claiming to be God and you write what God/GUS asks you to write?" inquired Detective Stewart.

"Yes, that's right. I know it sounds strange, but that is the truth."

The detectives looked at each other and then back at him.

"Well, this is no more strange than what you hear many ministers claim, is it?"

"Chief Parker says you are a trustworthy guy and he says if you say God/GUS is talking to you directly then we better assume that is the truth."

"So, why did this guy want to shoot me?" said Fred.

"They say they are from some kind of Fundamentalist Church group and you are the Devil. They were sent by God to kill you, they claim."

"They were not sent by me!" came a booming voice from somewhere in the room.

"What was that?" said both detectives in unison.

"It is I, GUS, and I want you to do everything in your power to make sure Fred and his wife Jenny are safe. Since when has God/I/GUS hired hit men to silence my detractors?"

"Yes, Sir," they both stood up at attention. They both looked very scared.

"Sit down, you two. I want to have a few words with you."

"Yes, sir, God, or whoever you are."

"I want you to do whatever you can to disavow Fred as the author. I want you to make sure he is safe until this passes. I have come to talk to my people and some do not like what I have to say."

"Yes, sir," replied Detective Stewart.

"Do you have any questions?" asked GUS.

About an hour later they both left very changed human beings. They vowed to protect Fred and Jenny and that they would both find the quiet space to talk to GUS when they got home.

"Are you all right Fred?" GUS said after the two detectives had gone.

"Yes, I am but I could hardly contain myself watching the two of them try to converse with you when they can't even see you."

"Yes, it must have been an odd sight," admitted GUS.

"Fred, it is good to see that your sense of humor is still working.

GUS said, "I visited the two in jail this morning and they are all right, but now are confused because I talked to them and they had their belief system upended.

"These two need some help, but shooting a police officer will cause them to be in lots of trouble. By the way, the officer will be fine.

"Let's take the morning off, Fred. Is that all right with you? I want you go pick up Jenny at her office and let her know what is going on. Let her know she will be safe."

"I'm leaving now," and Fred was gone.

CHAPTER 14

The next day Fred and GUS met back at Fred's place to continue the writing.

"How is Jenny and how are you?" was GUS's first question.

"Jenny is a little anxious and she told her employees some of what is going on so everyone could be alert to anything that seemed to be of concern or out of the ordinary.

Fred continued, "I feel a little anxious myself but I trust in You to keep an eye on me."

"I wish this was not going on, but, since it is, I have been thinking I may have to do more than just pass my messages through you. I have not decided what that will be yet." replied GUS.

"Do you want some human feedback?"

"Yes, I would appreciate your thoughts."

"I think that what you have to say should eventually be on the front page of every newspaper and across the web around the globe. Then everyone will get the facts straight from you.

"I feel however, that while there will be a time for that; for now, those that are drawn to what you have to say need a more personal way to tune in.

"My suggestion is that we move the "Thoughts Section" off my blog and create your blog as a separate site that anyone can come to and make comments. That will open the dialogue doorway.

"I'm sure we don't want to spend all of our days responding. I suggest comments can be made as time allows, but replies would not be part of the process for you."

"I think you are onto something and it will take the focus off you and put it on me," GUS enthusiastically responded.

"Exactly. I have enough website savvy that I can create a simple blog from an already formatted program. Then I will explore what it will take to make sure the blog can handle the traffic. I have a good friend I can consult with."

"All right, how much time do you need to put this together?"

"Give me until after midday tomorrow and we should be ready to roll," replied Fred.

"All right, that sounds like it will work. You are so appreciated Fred, for hanging in there as the human confusion flares up. You took the time to come up with a good idea for how to transition this away from you."

"Thanks."

"One other idea for my own blog. I would like to call it either, *The Blog Of Light* or *The World According To GUS*. Which do you recommend?"

"I like both names but *The World According To GUS* seems more fitting in a straight forward kind of way." Fred then paused and said, "The challenge will be to come up with a good image for the masthead."

"Masthead?" inquired GUS.

"Yes, the masthead is the picture, image, message across the top of the blog."

"I understand. I will leave that up to you, Fred. But I may send you inspiration to assist you. If you have questions, just ask."

"I mostly certainly will."

"I would like to have you post one message for today's blog.

Are you up for that?"

Fred said, "Yes, let's go."

"I have received some disturbing news about people thinking my blog writer is evil or the devil or something equally inaccurate. I am the writer of this Blog. I Am called God by many and a host of other names. I assure you that I Am who I say I Am. And to all I will now be called GUS.

"Do not attempt to hurt or in any way interfere with my partner in this who is simply using his hands to do the writing. Those that would do harm to him would do harm to me.

"If you are in fact upset with what I Am saying, talk to others and find the way back to your heart. I Am about love. I share all that I share from the place of love.

"If I question your institutions, it is because they need to be questioned. If I question your beliefs, it is because they need to be questioned.

"I want to make it very clear that I do all of this from a place of love. I have come to do this because for too long, too many have been acting as if they speak for me. Those pretenders have gotten too much power because people have given it to them. They do not speak for me, only I do.

"Please take some time to sort through what I am saying, ask questions, and get together with friends and talk. If you have a way that you tune inward for guidance, do that and listen deeply.

"Those that are outraged are so, because they have been questioned and they have been called on the carpet. This has never been a personal attack. I simply want to wake people up and to share the truth of who I Am.

"If people feel attacked, then it is time for self-examination. Defensiveness is evidence that a further exploration of self is needed.

"Most of all, please do this from a place of love. Love is the best path to finding the way to your truth. This is a time for personal awareness with a kind heart.

"I am protecting the name of my writer to keep his life safe. There were two people intent on killing him last night. Think of how wrong that thinking and reactivity is from my viewpoint.

"What kind of confused thinking would make it all right to kill another for what he is writing about, even if it puts your beliefs into question?

"This writing is a gift and an invitation to awaken. Those who see it as a threat are missing the point and are in fear and anger because they don't like feeling out of control.

"My writer friend is creating a new blog site for me and it will be up tomorrow. The working name for it will be *The World According To GUS*. I Am using the name GUS because it takes me away from all the misspoken words claimed in God's name. I Am not this false God so many say they speak for.

"There will be information later at this location that will direct you to the new blog's location.

"One more reminder, if you want to talk with me, it is very simple. All you have to do is find the quiet place inside you and be open to conversing with me. You will know me because I am the voice of the heart, of compassion, kindness and of reason."

That afternoon Fred completed a simply formatted blog and got it registered and hosted at a site that could deal with a lot of traffic. He was excited about this new direct approach because he felt many more would get to share in all the inspiration he'd received from his conversations with GUS.

The rest of the day he stayed close to home and enjoyed a surprisingly nice day for this time of year. The fall season in the Pacific Northwest is great for ducks, but too often, not so great for humans who get tired of the rain.

PART 2

The Blog
According to GUS

CHAPTER 15

The next day, GUS was very pleased with the new blog. "Thanks Fred, the blog looks good and the masthead is just what I had in mind."

They both smiled in appreciation for the work Fred had done.

"Now, Fred, all the people can find out more about my ways by coming directly to *The World According To GUS*."

"Yes, I think this will work well and those that have been following your words have the web address of the new site. I suspect your web address will be available to everyone in just a matter of a few days."

"All right Fred, lets get rolling."

"I'm ready and waiting."

"I wanted to start my first day at *The World According To GUS* with some of the ideas I have about how humans can get the most out of their lives using the gifts I have given them.

"Let's start with the human body. This is a beautiful creation with such an economy of design and function. I have given you a body that can see, hear, speak, taste, touch, smell, feel and sense. These abilities offer you so many possibilities.

"You can write and sing music. You can create, taste and enjoy wonderful meals. You can hear someone say, 'I love you'. You can learn to touch in healing ways. You can see the beauty of nature and hear the sounds of a stream. You can taste a fresh raspberry.

GUS continued, "You can hug someone while they cry their way through grief. You can ski down a mountain or surf a wave with the use of your eyes to see, your nose to smell, your ears to hear and your voice to shout with pleasure.

"This body has organs that make you tick, allow you to hold your breath, digest spicy foods, shoot energy through your system, regulate your functioning and so much more. The legs and feet and the arms and hands allow you to be able to play tennis, walk or run a marathon, do complicated surgery, write a book, play a violin, hold a baby, swing a bat or fly through the air on a swing.

"Your body is your feeling center — the place where you sense what is going on. Your heart is both a beating organ and the center of love. Fear raises the hair on your neck. Trouble knots up your stomach. Tension raises your shoulders. Joy dances across your smiling face.

"The feeling feedback your body gives you is an impeccable guidance system that always lets you know whether you are heading to or away from what you want in your life.

"The body is the place where your mind resides, your soul hangs out and your actions for success originate.

"I see the body as a temple where the highest and most sacred potential resides. It is a temporary place because who you are will pass on someday.

"However, the body needs to be treated well along the way for optimal functioning. Good doses of love, activities that keep you fit, all the needed rest you can get and laughter to keep the vibrations high are required. When the body is treated with respect, you can better count on it in the later years. Those are the times when your body's power may be less, but the power of your mind and heart are in full blossom.

"A healthy body is a simple matter in most cases, because if it is nurtured and cared for, it will serve you well. Within every one of my creations, I have placed a self-healing system that works best in a cared for body. The natural immunity and disease fighting attributes take over when needed.

"You can heal yourself of anything. Do not pay attention to any expert who says that is not true. There is within you the power of the mind, heart and spirit; the same healing powers that are in me.

"I hope this gives you a sense of how much you have been given to make your life a joy to live. Appreciating who you are and all you have will open you to realizing the greatest benefits of my gifts to you.

"Fred, how do you respond to these ideas? Am I lecturing too much?"

"No, not at all. As a matter of fact, I thought the images you created were ones people could feel as they read along."

"I do feel great passion when I speak about my creations and their gifts. I get excited about all that they have inside to make their lives work in positive ways!"

"I appreciate what you are saying. You seem so full of joy when you share what is possible in each human," said Fred.

"Fred, I agree. Yet lately, I have felt some doubt. This doubt is something I have never really encountered before."

"GUS has doubt?"

They laughed for it struck both of them as kind of funny that GUS would have doubt.

"In all seriousness, Fred, this doubt has come about since the incident at the game. I have been wondering if I have made a mistake reaching out to share who I Am with people. I came to help humans move forward, to expand their viewpoints and to move past limiting beliefs. Now, I wonder if all these questions have been too unsettling and have thrown my people too far off balance."

Fred quickly responded. "Your human creations are amazingly adaptive, maybe even at times to their detriment. So now you wonder if they wouldn't be better if you had remained in the background?"

"No, not really. It is disconcerting however, that some would try to harm those who are doing no harm. You are just writing for me. You are not telling them what to believe.

"I understand that some people seem to feel very threatened by being questioned. That alone is baffling to me. And then, for them to attempt to kill someone else because they feel threatened by ideas that are different from their own seems so clearly wrong.

"Now that I think about it, human history is full of these kind of inappropriate responses. I continue to hope that humans will evolve past this very primitive way of thinking and responding to different ideas.

"How did they become so fragile that other ideas are threatening? Why did many humans evolve to such a weak state of mind?

"Fred, a lot of questions have been coming up since the other night. I am concerned that the questioning may be too much for those who seem so inflexible in their thinking."

"GUS, this is confusing to me, too. I hope after a period of deeper understanding that human minds more fully expand into what you and I have talked about — the higher mind guided by the heart and the soul."

GUS continued, "I appreciate that people are very adaptive however, it can lead to a denial of self that is stifling. How many have settled for so much less because they have rationalized doing so? How many have not paid attention to what is going on inside because it is easier to ignore? How many are so caught up in the circumstances of their upbringing that they don't even know they have other options? How many feel they want something better but they just don't know how to get there? There are so many questions to be asked.

"You know, Fred, life is just one big huge experiment that each person tries to make the best of. I see that those who go for more in life and stretch themselves to be all they can be are the ones that seem to have the best time.

"Those that just make do and take it easy can also enjoy the journey, but too often the simple becomes complex and disrupts all of life. Then self-doubt creeps in. I wish I could make everything work out great for everyone all the time, but freedom of choice rules and many choices are made that come from mistaken thinking rather than from their deeper wisdom."

"Yes, I wish you could wave your magic wand and everyone would live happily ever after, but that is not the freedom of choice, which you believe important for everyone," responded Fred.

"Yes, freedom of choice is essential for humans to evolve. Without that choice, then it is me shaping the world I want and humans become like pawns in a game rather than conscious beings determining their lives.

"Well, it is time to take a break for lunch, Fred."

"Yes, it is and Jenny and I have a date."

"I remembered. I thought I would stop by her office and have a visit with her staff. They are doing such courageous work that I wanted to cheer them on. I will go there now and see you when you arrive to pick up Jenny."

GUS was gone in a flash as Fred quickly looked to see if

comments were happening on the new blog site. There were 1305 comments already, even before the first official post. Fred transferred all the GUS guided posts from *Sports Heaven* to *The World According To GUS*.

People had plenty to say and he was glad the comments were meant for GUS and not for him. After the shooting, the negative comments directed at Fred had mostly gone away. He guessed it was because too many must have felt some part of themselves in the shooter or maybe GUS's message of love was truly gaining traction."

When Fred arrived at Jenny's, the place was electric with conversation as GUS responded to question after question.

"Yes, I know, the Bible has been seen as precious by so many people. It is still a wonderful collection of stories that can be helpful for those that read it. It is not just 'the word of God or GUS.'

"My writings through Fred are the very first words from GUS to the people of Earth. Sure, others have been inspired by their relationship with me and have written with wisdom, but they never wrote for me.

"I am sure my discussion of the Bible is stirring up a lot of reaction and hopefully, some positive and expansive thinking.

"I have decided to reach out to my precious humans because I am concerned that who I Am has gotten hidden in a cloud of misrepresentation. There are many who say they speak for me, but they do not. All religion and all churches are the inventions of the human mind. Some of these human inventions have been of great service to humanity.

"I have no religion and those that say their religion is the only way to me are completely wrong.

"Another reason I have come forward now is to make it clear

that churches and religions are big businesses and that is not part of my plan. These organizations are all part of human plans.

"Humans have free choice to make plans or create whatever organizations they want. They have no right however, to say they represent me because they do not. All the powers of these organizations and churches granted to humans from the Bible and other sources were granted to them from other humans, not from me. I have never authorized any church to exist in my name.

"I can tell by your questions that most of you have been reading my blog. I am so glad you feel comfortable enough to ask me what concerns you.

"I find myself wanting to emphasize several points of view here. The idea of eternal damnation is a human creation to control people. Original sin is a human creation to control people. Fear used by your government is a human tool used to control people.

"All of these are human inventions or ideas and the world will be a better place if you can remember that it is human manipulation that is going on.

"I am a loving GUS that sees you as you are and loves you fully and completely. The idea of hell is just a human idea.

"Often people ask where you go after you die. That is simple for me to answer. You return to me. You and I are one. When you die you return to the full realization of that oneness.

"In your world very few are open in mind and heart enough to know the truth of our oneness. This is because the limiting ideas you grew up with keep the idea of total unity buried under a pile of self-doubts and misunderstandings.

"Did that answer your questions? I want you all to know that there is in you the same light that is in me. There is in all of you the full capacity that is in me. The goal of your life, from

My perspective, is to fully express who you are and realize your divine nature."

The question and answer session went on for several hours.

Then GUS said, "All right that is enough information to spin around in your head for now."

"Will you visit us again?" asked several of Jenny's co-workers.

"Yes, I will come back.

"At this point though, I am unsure how much I will reach out to other gatherings of people. I will continue to write through Fred. The rest of this process of my connecting to humans appears to be unfolding as it goes.

"I Am grateful for this time to have direct contact with all of you. I feel enriched by this and I want to remind you that I Am always available to you if you take the time to be quiet and listen. I may come in the form of an inner voice, a deep sense of true knowing, a message from the heart, your soul or other channels that communicate with you in ways by which you can receive me. Please contact me often. Goodbye."

They all sat in silence for what seemed like a long time. Then they gathered around Jenny and Fred and soaked up the love and light filling the room. Each was profoundly affected.

CHAPTER 16

F red made his way back home later in the afternoon and there his 'blogger buddy' was waiting for him.

"You know, Fred, I am finding out how much I love direct and in person contact with people. I had always kept some distance, like a parent trying not to over-parent. I did not want to influence their decisions and wanted to let them just be who they are. This way there has been lots of exploring and discovering. I have watched the whole process unfold.

"Now, I see their choices have been disrupted by all those that falsely claim to know the truth. In other words, the power of human programming by society has blocked the natural evolutionary process in some ways. I want to set that process back on track.

"Would you write what I just said for the blog? I think I am changing directions somewhat because my contact with people is informing my decisions.

"I want people to know that this coming out on my part is evolving as I learn from my conversations with the people I Am meeting. The individual seeds of awakening are in need of nurturing and I am doing the groundwork that will encourage these seeds to grow.

"This blog is part one of the groundwork. My interacting directly with others is part two. I suspect part three will involve a way to directly interact with much larger groups of people.

"Please include these ideas in the blog today. I genuinely want those tuning in to know that I Am sincere in my desire to be experienced as reachable and available to all.

"Will this make sense to people, Fred?"

"Yes, it will. I am excited that your word is spreading and that people are being stirred. Will you change into some kind of human form?"

"No, I will not, because human history tells me that my form would be in danger by forces that are more interested in their story than they are in mine.

"I am beginning to see a mass awakening is possible and I may want to encourage and inspire that to happen.

"Today, I want you to add some more to the blog. Are you ready to go on, Fred?"

"Yes, GUS, I look forward to sharing what you have to say and to learning from your wisdom."

GUS began, "I have been thinking about truth and what it is. I know truth because I see the whole picture and seeing the whole picture is very informative. When you don't have the whole picture you rely too much on other people's perspectives. I Am here now to share the whole picture from my viewpoint. Then all will be fully informed.

"I Am feeling good about all that I Am sharing. I Am however, starting to understand that this kind of lecture style via the blog may not be the best format.

"The interaction I had with Jenny's employees taught me that I love being in close contact. I love hearing their questions and concerns and being able to directly respond to them. That feels most alive to me. I must admit to being surprised by the joy I feel in those kinds of exchanges.

"Before coming here to work with you, I had never interacted in such a direct and verbal way with humans other than in the silence of prayer and in intimate communications with those who knew how to speak directly to me. What I Am doing here is allowing me to learn about myself and how wonderful human beings can be. I didn't know there was more for me to learn in this way, but there definitely is."

Fred said, "I find this whole exploration full of such aliveness and I am deeply touched by the sharing we have going on here."

"Fred, I like the aliveness and dynamic part of this whole unfolding too."

"Are you winding down the blog idea then?"

"No, not at all. The blog is a great way for me to share a variety of ideas.

I do want to increase my contact with small groups though and I Am considering ways to meet with larger groups that would also be interactive."

Fred suggested, "The words that come to my mind immediately are *town hall meetings*. This however, would involve way too many meetings to reach out to everyone, wouldn't it?"

"Fred, you may not have taken an important fact into consideration. I can be in more than one place at a time. As a matter of fact, I could be in all places at once responding to all questions."

"Wow, of course You can. I never even imagined that was possible."

That afternoon the two of them put together a plan for community-based meetings all over the world.

"Two weeks from Sunday at twelve noon, wherever you can gather in your community, GUS will show up and respond to your questions. GUS welcomes churches and other communities to join in."

The World According To GUS was the first place where this announcement was made about the direct local visits with GUS. The reaction was swift as the word spread across the Web in just hours. The "Comments" section was filled with responses from all over the world asking GUS to visit.

From that day on, GUS's blog was the most popular site on the Web. There was so much excitement about the upcoming visits with GUS. The blog kept providing the readers with the words of GUS and the latest updates about everyone who wanted GUS to come to their communities.

CHAPTER 17

———————

"Fred, I think we've gotten the whole world stirred up. I feel very positive about all the dialogue that is going on. The comments are very supportive in general, aren't they, Fred?"

"Yes, they are. I have been keeping track of some of the more interesting responses and wanted to tell you about them.

"I heard from three churches that have turned their organizations into human service centers and are awaiting further guidance. I have had numerous churches offering you a permanent residence at their location. I have a group of nuns who are asking if they can become priests under your direction.

"I have a Muslim organization requesting your help with writing a Koran that is accurate. Two Bible scholars have offered to co-author a revised Bible.

"I even heard from a Zen monk who invited you to come to a gathering to speak with his Buddhist community.

"There are thousands of responses that are as interesting as the ones I just shared with you."

Then the two of them spent several hours responding to questions and comments.

"Thanks for keeping me informed and for organizing all of this, Fred."

"I love doing this," was Fred's exuberant reply!

"I was thinking that if churches did want to get involved, they could have study groups about what I Am sharing. The GUS Collection would serve as a reference with my real words stated very clearly and with no interpretation necessary."

Fred enthusiastically said, "I really appreciate what you are thinking and you are giving those church communities a way to continue to exist. I suspect that a good number of those organizations do attempt to serve their members with compassion and kindness."

"That is right, Fred, communities coming together to explore the truth fits perfectly with what churches can do to make a positive difference in the world.

"I suggest we take the rest of the day off. I have more to say but the context is changing so I want to get clearer myself as to what makes the most sense."

"GUS, I can feel the energy of all of this and I sense a hugely positive response."

"Fred, your trust of your intuitive knowing is allowing you to better express your potential. I feel so joyous watching you grow as we work together."

"Thank you, GUS, I am filled with appreciation for all that you have encouraged in me. I feel so good when I am with you."

"You are welcome, Fred. All right let us break or we will go on and on. I will see you tomorrow mid morning."

"I'll be here and ready to be of service."

Later that evening after the game that Fred was covering, he was confronted by a small gathering of people. They knew who he was and about the blog he had been writing.

"How can you do what you are doing and lie to people and say you are God?" one of them demanded.

"In the first place I am not lying, and second, your tone is threatening and I will not stand here and put up with it," responded Fred firmly.

"Sorry, we didn't mean to come on so strong. We are just upset about what the blog says and we think you should reconsider doing it."

"So, you are telling me to stop doing what GUS has asked me to do?" questioned Fred.

"There is no God involved, be honest with us."

"I am being totally and completely honest with you."

Then the voice was there and panic appeared on their faces.

"Do not be afraid, but listen to what I have to say."

"Where is that coming from?" the apparent spokesperson said to the others.

"It is coming from GUS. You are doubters of my word, I take it?"

"No, we are believers, but you cannot be GUS because our religion says you do not appear to your people."

"Then, if I were you, I would question what your religion teaches."

The conversation lasted about 30 minutes and the people left surprised and excited by the encounter.

"Fred, are you all right?" inquired GUS.

"Yes, I am. I think those guys are going to have to rethink a whole lot of what they thought was the truth."

"Yes, they are and the more I Am out in the world, the more that truth seeking is going to happen."

"I'll see you tomorrow and thanks for watching out for me."

"Of course, I must. We still have important things to do."

The next day GUS showed up and as always, checked in with Fred. Fred was doing well, so they started working right away.

"Today I wanted to share some ideas about guilt. This is

one of the worst of all the human emotions because it is falsely taught to be real. Those that want you to feel bad about who you are have used guilt for centuries.

"Guilt is a learned human emotion and is often used solely for manipulation. Churches, organizations, political parties and all other ego-based organizations have used guilt for the purpose of creating doubt in the individual. Self-doubt makes a person easy to manipulate and easy to control.

"Guilt is an entirely human invention, which from my viewpoint serves no positive purpose. Guilt doesn't make a person change their behavior; it just makes them feel guilty. When people feel guilty they lose confidence in their ability to make good decisions for themselves. Guilt is an effective technique for disempowering people.

"My recommendation is to say goodbye to guilt. Stop feeling guilty about who you are and what you are doing. If someone is attempting to make you feel guilty, kindly tell him or her that you don't believe in guilt. If you are making yourself feel guilty, tell yourself to stop because you don't believe in guilt.

"I know that what I speak about here goes against the teachings of many churches. That is why I am sharing it, in order to teach a greater truth.

"You do not have to ever feel guilty unless you want to. I suspect many would rather just do things differently than feel guilty. Stop feeling guilty, align with what you know is right for you and free yourself to be all right with who you are and how you are in the world.

"Fred, how are you doing? You look like this hit home for you."

"I am thinking about how much guilt training I got going to a religious school. They regularly read us all the sins we could be committing and told us all the things we were doing wrong. They tried to make us feel guilty just for being human.

I have spent a long time working on letting all that guilt go. I am grateful for your view on this because that letting go process for me has now finally ended. I am free. I see no reason to feel guilty anymore. I am going to choose other, more supportive emotions."

"Fred, I like the way you said that. 'You are going to choose other, more supportive emotions.' Yes, your emotional state is almost always a matter of the thoughts you have. Change your thinking and you change your experience. I know that is said over and over again by self-help writers and teachers. They are 100% right about that."

"I have been learning so much from you, GUS. This 'leaving guilt behind' is something I may have needed to hear more than anything else. Guilt has made me feel lousy for too long. I can change how I feel, how I experience my life and the world, by simply changing the way I think. The mind is an amazing creator, isn't it?"

"Yes, my hope in being here and sharing so many ideas is to assist everyone in realizing the expansive nature of their minds. You **are** your thoughts.

"In a very simple way, **all you have to do is think and feel your life as you want it to be and it will become extraordinary.** I promise that to you."

"I am getting this down, GUS. To me, this is something every human being needs to understand if they want to have a good life."

"Not only a good life, Fred, but a masterpiece of individual expression and realization.

"Ready for a break now, Fred?"

"Yes, I feel the urge to move my body and breathe some fresh air. I'll go up into the West Hills and run some trails. You are welcome to join me."

"I will pass this time. I feel I Am needed someplace and I must go now," and just like that, GUS was gone.

That afternoon Fred read about a massive earthquake in East Asia. He read also there would be a tidal wave that could cause much suffering. Fred wondered if GUS went there. He'd ask the next time they were together.

CHAPTER 18

Fred and GUS were back at work the next day and Fred asked if GUS had been where the earthquake had happened.

"Fred, how did you know?"

"I could sense you being there."

"I was there and I actually talked to a number of those who were afraid. I told them who I was and that they would be all right. I was so touched by their genuineness as people and by their compassion for each other.

"I also dissipated the wave before it caused additional damage. It was what they requested, so I was more than glad to assist them.

"After their safety was assured, we got together and talked and they all seemed so grateful for the conversation. They requested I visit them again soon. I promised I would be back in a week or so. I will be there for the worldwide conversation because they were very clear they wanted me there.

"I am getting such a loving response from so many that it is a real pleasure for me to be interacting so directly with people. I am looking forward to the worldwide conversation in about 10 days. There is so much I want to share.

"As I read what you write, Fred, I see that I say my people often. I have a deep respect for the human journey and I want to make it clear that I do not say my people in a possessive way but more in awe in the way good parents feel when they see their children thrive."

Fred assured GUS, "I understand the tone of how you say *my* with such love and I am sure the readers will now clearly understand it comes from love."

"Tone? You are right, Fred, tone in words on a paper or screen can be less than clear. I hadn't really thought of that. Nice assist on your part. Thanks and thank you for being such a great partner for me on this coming out party."

"You are welcome. It is with deep joy that I get to be a part of this extraordinary event that will surely transform humanity."

"I hope you are right, Fred, about the positive impact. Actually I Am sure this thing we are doing will make a big difference."

"Are you ready to get back at it?" asked Fred.

"Yes, I am.

"I was thinking, Fred, that I want to write today about who I Am and how I see the relationship between myself and those that want to interact with me."

"That sounds like a good idea."

"Oh, by the way, how are the comments going?"

"They have gotten increasingly positive and supportive of you coming out and sharing your ideas. There are still those that seem angry about what you are saying, but even those groups are less nasty in what they write. We got a response yesterday from a minister in Ohio that said he is confused now about what to do and how to take his ministry forward after reading the blog. I wrote him back and said I would tell you of his questions."

"Yes, I know who you are talking about. He decided to follow my guidance and spent time being quiet and listening for my response to his questions. He is now moving forward and changing his ministry to what he refers to as the *call of love* and he will dedicate his work to spreading love in the world.

"He is going to propose to his church that together they all commit to spreading love and turn the church into more of a community of spiritual seekers doing good works. We both anticipated that would go over well with the many good people he has worked with for over 25 years."

"That is good news," said Fred. "He seemed so heartfelt in his questions."

"Yes, he is, and that is one reason I thought about talking more about who I Am and how we can grow our relationships with each other. What I want to do is to emphasize some of what I have shared already and hopefully bring more understanding.

"The first and most important sharing I have, is to again state that I Am a loving force. I Am not someone to be afraid of or for you to worry about how I might feel about you. I Am very understanding and compassionate towards everyone. I want you to realize that my love for each of you is unlimited and not affected by what you think, say or do.

"I do not listen in on your life nor do I watch to make sure you are acting right. I Am not interested in being a monitor for your behavior. That is a human idea of a God that has nothing better to do then sit in judgment over everyone. That is a totally false idea and needs to be wiped out of the human mind.

"I have come to Earth now because I want to share my larger perspective. What needs clarification is that all that has been said in my name is inaccurate. That is a huge amount of misinformation. I Am not blaming anyone nor am I angry about the misinformation.

"I just want you to be informed about the bigger picture so you can more freely shape your life. If you read through the blog you will see all that I have said and all that is my truth. I am grateful to my friend who has spelled this all out for me.

"I am not here to condemn anyone nor what they do. I have come to make things clear so the misinformation can stop. All that has been said about me confuses so many people.

"I realize that my words about the Bible have been in direct contradiction to what most have said and heard. The Bible is not made up of my words. Its words were created entirely by your fellow humans. The stories in the Bible are not fact, they are stories made up by men, many years ago.

"I Am not sure how it got to be considered such a sacred book, but it has wrongly become much more than it is. I recommend that the book be put on the shelf and that people start to talk to each other and to me and together we can create a world that will nurture the spirit in everyone.

"Ministers, priests, imam, monks and rabbis have represented me, not on my authority, but on a kind of false self authority. They are not bad for doing this, just mistaken. I Am not upset with them for most were just following the guidance of those who they thought knew the truth. That is often the problem with following the guidance of those you think know; you get lead falsely.

"You do not need to be lead falsely anymore. If you choose you can now be guided by me by developing your own relationship with me. I will continue to share more about that as we go.

"I Am not in human form. I can be heard but not seen. I have my friend assisting me so that I can put these words onto this screen for you to read.

"I Am neither male nor female. I Am not a body, but more of a thinking and sensing field of energy and consciousness. My heart is the Universe, which has beat with aliveness since the beginning and will continue for eternity. My love extends into every particle everywhere. I love all beings everywhere without conditions.

"Yes, there are multiple universes and all of them are contained in me. There are other planets like Earth elsewhere. There are other beings, but that is another story and I will not address that now.

"I want you to know I have a sense of humor. I feel for what goes on in your world. I want the best for you. You have been equipped with all that you need to create a wonderful life for yourself and those you care about. Each person on Earth is filled with the highest and best qualities. You are made with all my abilities except you have a human form.

"I Am infinite and without limits. I created evolution and I let it proceed, as it does, naturally. I Am a reflection of the highest consciousness and my wisdom is the highest of all that is known. This all sounds like I Am some kind of hotshot. I am neither hotshot nor humble. I Am all things.

I Am harmony and balance in perfect form. I have been called by many names. God is most familiar, but there are many other names humans have used to describe me like Allah, Yahweh, Great Spirit, the Tao, Krishna, Source, Divine Mother, Holy Father, Sacred Heart, Alpha, Omega, and more. I Am none of those names. I Am nameless, yet I will gladly respond to whatever you call me, as long as it is done with a desire to have a relationship with me.

"The name GUS was chosen because it was free of all the other false misinformation. GUS stands for God, Great Spirit, Guidance — Universe, Universal Mind, Unity Consciousness — Source, Spirit, Soul. Please feel free to call me GUS if you like.

"I could go on, but I suspect that is enough information about who I Am for now. I hope this is making sense to all of you. I will share more about my nature in our future conversations.

"The second part of this sharing is about what kind of relationship is possible between you and me. First, you can reach out to me through your heart in quiet prayer, meditation or by just requesting guidance.

"Please call me what you feel comfortable with. I will call you by your name unless you want to be called something else.

"The way to have a relationship with me is to spend time in conversation. I suggest, as I have written before, the best way to do that is to find your inner stillness and then begin to ask the questions and seek the guidance you want. Then wait for my response. I always respond. It may take you a few times to get the feel for tuning in and listening.

"Listening is a very key component. Without listening deeply, there is only the noise of your mind at work. Once we open a channel, the conversations will flow. I would love to have a relationship with every person on the planet.

"Some may find it helpful to have a notebook when we converse. It can be useful to write our conversation down for two reasons.

One reason is that the mind can be so confusing, but when you write our conversations down, then we get clearer because they are in written form. Another reason to consider writing our conversations out is because you can review them and ask further questions later.

"I want to make it clear that you do not have to communicate with me. You can go about your life in any way you want. If you don't see a place in your life for me, I have no issue with that. You have free choice and no one is ever condemned by me for their choices. I respectfully allow you to be who you are and live the life you want.

"I Am not hurt if you choose to live without me in your life. I still want the best for you but I Am not able to help guide you if you do not want to relate to me. I Am here to encourage your fullest expression of who you are, to cheer you on and even guide you toward a life of satisfying self-realization. The guidance is optional. That is your choice.

"The exception to this basic plan of non-intervention, unless requested, is happening now through the blog and my worldwide meetings to come. I have broken with my plan for the reasons explained previously. I am taking a more active role temporarily and then will return to my previous non-intervention approach.

"It is my hope that my coming forward will help expand my personal relationship with all beings on the planet. The animals and all other creatures have always lived in harmony with me. I hope humans come into a more expanded experience of me, so they, too, can find balance and harmony.

"You and I are one. I Am in this moment and every moment, available to you. There are no limits to what we can create together. I invite you to explore the possibilities and together we can turn this planet into a place that will encourage and inspire the best in everyone.

"Please, if you have any questions, find the place in you where we both reside and then talk with me and listen and I will be there for you. The potential for how we can relate is unlimited. I am complete for now. I will be in touch with you soon.

"Fred, sorry, that was a long one. How are you doing?"

"I am feeling renewed and energized," replied Fred.

"Excellent, should we go for a walk and talk?"

"Yes, I would like that very much."

They left Fred's house and were gone for many hours. What they talked about was just between GUS and Fred and that was a beautiful thing.

CHAPTER 19

The Blog remained silent for several days as far as new posts were concerned, but the comments were flowing in steadily, and people were beginning to be worried that GUS had left.

"Well, the time is coming near, Fred, for my big meeting. There are some further things I want to share before then."

"GUS, before you do, I was checking the comments and people are worried because they have not seen a blog posting in several days."

"Yes, I was afraid that would happen. I suggest that you post a brief note and say that if anyone wants to make contact with me, please do so on our *one-to-one* channel.

"The blog is a great way to communicate, but I will not be a blogger for that much longer, so their relationship with me needs to be on a personal basis."

Fred took a few minutes to do a quick post reporting what GUS had asked him to write.

"Okay, I've posted the message on the blog and told them that more blogging would be happening later today."

"Good job. Are you ready to roll?"

"Yes, I am," responded Fred.

"The topic I wanted to share today has to do with personal empowerment and creating the life you want. The first point I want to make clear is that only you are responsible for creating your life.

"No one, not even me, is responsible for making your life what it is. That is not to say I will not aid you as you go, but even my assistance only comes at your request. The more you take full responsibility for your life, the more your life will feel like you are making it happen. That is human empowerment. That is the human experiment.

"I gave you the ability to make your life what you want it to be. If you get clear about what you want, hold it in your thoughts and your heart, are open to having it and take the necessary steps to make it happen — it will happen.

"You have everything that you need to fully succeed in all aspects of your life. Those that have written and spoken about the importance of having an intention and putting your attention on it wrote with clarity.

"What gets in your way of being fully empowered and empowering others is always **you** — period. If you are a student of insight and awareness you can take this information and learn so much about how you get in your own way.

"The only thing that can hamper your path to success is you. That makes other people and circumstances ultimately irrelevant. Certainly, other people and circumstances can offer challenges, but human history has shown that people are able to win out even in the most difficult of situations.

"The human spirit is simply unlimited. The only limits are the ones you place on yourself. I never place any limits on you. Most limits develop from your thoughts through what you learned from your family and the world you live in. Unnecessary limitations have been passed on for generations.

"That can cease to happen as soon as you become aware

and make different choices. In each moment, if you can be 'in awareness', you can choose to be run by your limitations or to be free to be your own unlimited self. It all comes back to responsibility. When you decide to take responsibility, you take full charge of your life.

"Those that say they give their lives over to me are those unwilling to take full responsibility for their own life. 'I give my life to God' is not something that I have asked for or that I even think is a good idea. Those that have a relationship with me know this to be true.

"I see nothing wrong with those who dedicate themselves to living by the highest spiritual principles. That is taking responsibility for your life and living by your highest values. This dedicated kind of life will have it's own rewards.

"Those that claim to live in my name but do not have a relationship with me are confused and are guided by faulty human principles. There are many such as these, who must seek clarity for they have lost themselves in confusion.

"I am available to everyone for guidance. I request that all those who want to live for me need to get to know me. Then, live according to the life they know inwardly is right for them. A life dedicated to unconscious obligation needs to be re-examined.

"I have always wanted the best for you and that can only come if you are a conscious, aware, loving and open human being. I can help you find that way.

"I want to write a word of caution here, because I have seen over and over again a human fault that gets in the way of creating a wonderful life. That fault is the opposite of self-responsibility. Its usual comes as double trouble — blaming and complaining.

"I know that every human being has most likely been involved in this troubled thinking at points in their life. That is all right. It is not a sin (nor is anything else a sin) to blame or to complain. It is simply an ineffective way to view the world. That viewpoint means very clearly that you don't feel you have any power over your circumstances.

"You are never powerless even though you may feel like it sometimes. You always have the power to choose how to respond to what is going on. You can look at it in multiple ways. Seeing yourself as powerless is only one option.

"Blaming and complaining are powerful because they usually cause you to have more to blame and complain about. These two discontents attract more of what you are focused on and life can be very uneasy when you are feeling so angry and powerless.

"The higher part of you that is in full alignment with me wants nothing to do with having things to complain about. Complaining labels yourself as a victim and that cannot feel good, does not empower you nor is it true.

"I have shared these ideas because so many of you are focused on things that do not seem to be working out very well. Remember about the power that is the result of where your attention is.

"If you focus on how wrong the government is, then you are stuck in complaining.

"If you are antiwar and angry, you are focused on blaming and there can be no peace from that place for you.

"If you hate paying taxes, then you are complaining and creating great discontent within.

"If you think about how wronged you have been by your parents or others, then you have given them all your power.

"None of this sounds like much fun, does it? It is not any fun nor in any way is it truly satisfying to blame the world for what **isn't** happening for you.

"Step up fully in your life and look directly at what is not working and ask yourself these questions:

- How do I make a positive difference here?
- How do I focus on solutions, rather than on what is not working?
- How do I empower myself in the situation by making course corrections or by doing something that will positively affect the outcome?

"I hope you find these ideas helpful. There are a number of conscious people on the planet that know these ideas and they are working to help wake people up so that everyone will be empowered. Learning from those that seem to have a higher understanding of things can be helpful, as long as you keep in mind that their knowing is also part of your knowing. Keep your own counsel as you go and visit with me if you want to know my views.

"Fred, how are you doing?"

"This is so much good advice and for most of us these higher understandings will take some time to fully integrate into our lives," responded Fred.

"Yes, I agree Fred, time will be needed. That is why I am having you write this down so it can serve as a reminder. The integration part often takes time. Moving from old ways to new ways takes patience and persistence.

"I know this is much to think about. Let us break for today."

"I agree," said Fred.

"How are things going, Fred, and how is Jenny and her work group?"

"She is doing great and so are we. Our love is really blossoming again and I feel so blessed by this love in my heart and also so blessed because of you. Jenny's work group has requested that you stop by again soon."

"Thanks for the gratitude and I do plan to stop by this week again. I Am especially happy to see and feel that heart of yours in full glow."

"Yes, it is a joy to be in this state."

"My highest dream for the planet and for my precious human beings is they all have the opportunity to experience much love and that the planet be a light to the whole universe because of all the love that is here.

"My hope is that humans will begin to tap into and understand the vast inner resources of love they have. There is no limit to how much love each person can give."

Fred says, "I really enjoy it when you talk about love. It makes my heart feel like it is glowing. Just talking about love is so uplifting. I'll put these words in the blog and spread your light."

"Thank you so much for opening so fully to love, Fred. Everyone has this capacity that you are showing and living. It feels so good for me to be around loving human beings. It makes me feel joy for all my people."

Fred and GUS talked for several hours about love and how Fred could be a powerful force for love on the planet. Fred was glowing with the passion and potential of love; his heart was expanding right in the moment.

CHAPTER 20

———————

Fred and GUS had begun to call the upcoming meeting with the whole world, "The Mass Awakening", because they both felt the power that was expanding moment by moment. This expansive energy was charged and capable of transforming everything that came into contact with it. Fred called this energy "GUS Consciousness."

"Fred, I think we need a plan for the meeting and I want you to help me get this in some kind of order."

"I will gladly assist you in any way that will be helpful. I agree a plan makes sense, but I doubt if it is necessary, because as always, you do what you do from such a place of knowing that you will be very spontaneous."

"I am sure you are right about that," agreed GUS.

Fred continued, "Two days from now, you are going to be very busy. At noon, wherever the people are gathered who have requested your presence, you will be there. Over a twenty-four hour period you will have meetings with people all over the planet.

"We have over 1,000,000 gatherings that have requested you visit them. The largest group is about 50,000 that will come together in a soccer stadium in Eastern Europe. The smallest gathering is a circle of 5 friends in Upper Minnesota.

Do you feel excited about this?" questioned Fred.

"Yes, I am feeling lots of energy and anticipation. I guess that is what you would call excitement. I never knew I could feel this way."

"So, this is a new experience for you?"

"Yes, it is Fred, and as I mentioned before, I feel very good about having new experiences. I am a life force that evolves just like those that I have created."

"You're also a being that seems capable of new insights and awareness," Fred pointed out.

"Yes, that is very observant on your part, Fred."

The next two days went by very quickly for Fred, as he was busy with his work and with responding to inquiries he had been getting since his blog section had created such a stir. People were acting as if **he** had something to say since he was GUS's right hand man.

He laughed at the attention and recommended to everyone that they find their own relationship with GUS.

GUS was busy too, since there were meetings happening with a number of groups already, as well as the promise to meet with Jenny's work group again.

This meeting with Jenny's staff was more energized and the questions were numerous and full of passion. Many had found the first meeting to be so powerful that they had taken the time to explore their relationship with GUS. They all enjoyed the group gathering because they could learn from each other's questions.

GUS responded to each question with caring and compassion. There were a number of questions from people that were seeking clarity about their relationship with GUS and how this relationship was going to affect their church going activities.

"Going to church is up to you. If you feel your soul is nurtured;

if you feel uplifted to take on the challenges of life; if you feel empowered and the church understands that it does not speak for me, then the church you attend may provide the kind of community that is beneficial for you. There is no obligation to go to church, even though many have tried to get you to think that. Only go if it meets your needs.

"I suspect some churches will experience financial problems because of what I say. Those that are truly beneficial will survive. I have only love for all those that have, in their own way, done their best. Many ministers fall into that category.

I suggest that ministers expand their work of caring and compassion and discontinue preaching in my name."

It just so happened that two of the 10 employees had husbands that worked as ministers. That is why so many questions were focused on churches and GUS understood their concerns.

When they were through asking questions and GUS was finished responding, GUS again said, "Please keep in contact with me and let me know how you are doing.

"I Am guessing that the world, as you know it, is on the verge of shifting to the higher wisdom of conscious people. All of you are such beautiful human beings that I recommend you step forward to help this shift take place. I am willing to guide anyone who is willing to ask me for help."

Jenny asked if there would be another chance for them to all get together.

"I do not know at this time. I am sensing that the work I came here to do is going to be accomplished in the next several months. If so, I may not be back."

"I hope you do return to visit us. I think I speak for everyone, you are always welcome here among us."

"I can feel that is true," answered GUS.

Then, an energy passed through the room, everyone felt uplifted in their hearts and spirits and GUS was gone.

That was not to be the last time GUS visited with Jenny and her staff. Each of them had developed personal relationships with GUS.

Each week they got together and shared what they were learning through their individual contacts. The group at Jenny's office would be the model for many other groups exploring together the new awareness that each was discovering.

The following Sunday everything changed in profound ways.

PART 3

The
Mass Awakening

CHAPTER 21

The meetings began at noon at different locations all over the planet. With over a million groups involved, GUS's attention would be divided as never before. Although this was a new experience, GUS was up to the task.

Fred had been granted a special viewing of it all, so he could write about it for those who would ask about this incredible day. He was able to attend meetings all over the planet instantaneously because GUS had him as a companion at one event every hour.

Fred experienced 24 hours that would change everything. How that was accomplished was kept between Fred and GUS.

This is what Fred reported.

GUS began each gathering with the following words.

"Hello, beautiful ones. I Am so grateful to be able to engage with you in this unique experience that I Am calling *Inviting the Divine in Everyone.* I have come before you to share some ideas and to help clarify who I am and what I know to be the truth from my perspective.

"I ask that you keep an open mind and heart as I share with you today. I do not ask that you accept everything I say without question. I only ask that you think about and feel what I share with you and then make up your own mind as to what to accept and what to explore further.

"I want to share four basic points and then I will be open to questions. Here are the points I have come to clarify for everyone:

"First and most important of all, is that I am a loving GUS who loves all beings no matter who they are, their color, their sexual orientation, their behavior, their beliefs or their religion. I have no favorites. I condemn no one. I take revenge on no one. There is no hell. I do not punish people. I only love you and wish for you to have the most amazing life. You deserve the best. I have created you as I am. You can do almost anything I can do. That sounds amazing and it is.

"Second, I have no religion. Religion is a human creation. Religion and churches have said much in my name. None of what they have said has ever been my words. The Bible is not the word of GUS; it is a collection of human stories written by my people. All the world's sacred texts are the words of humans, not my words. Religion has created numerous images of who I Am. None of those images is who I Am. I have come to make it clear to you all that the only way to have a relationship with me is through me.

"Third, all the wars and horrible things done in my name are human creations. I have not ever supported any war and I never will. All wars are murder and are about the human ego trying to have more power and control over others. Wars are human madness. I Am a peaceful GUS who believes that loving your neighbor is the solution to problems. All problems including terrorism, lack of security, out of control governments, greed driven businesses and every other problem can be resolved by people getting together to talk, seek understanding and have compassion and care for one another.

"Fourth, you are all here in this life to fully express who you are. You are not here to please me or anyone else. This life you have been given is about love, joy, and the purpose you feel inside. You have unlimited tools to succeed at whatever it is you know you are here to do. You are the only one that can be you. The highest wisdom I have heard from a human was the wise statement about how best to live your life, 'Follow your bliss'. I Am always available to you if you choose to seek my guidance.

"At this moment I feel so moved to be able to communicate with so many who want to communicate with me. I welcome any questions you have. I will remain with you until all your questions are answered. I do have new messages every hour but that will not stop me from being with you."

"Yes, Sun Yee, what is your question?" GUS called everyone by his or her name.

"Great teacher, what am I to believe about the teachings I have received by the ancient ones in my Taoist tradition?"

"These teaching represent the highest human understandings. The great Taoist mystics spent time in communion with nature and sometimes even with me in the quiet of their deep meditations. They were wise in their understanding of the way. See how what I say today fits with what they taught and what does not, and then come to your own conclusions." responded GUS.

"There is, in the West, this tradition called heaven and hell and the missionaries taught me about these two places. Do they exist?"

"Ben, they exist only as states you create here on earth. They are not places you go to after this life. The only heaven and hell is how you fashion your life. If you are negative, fearful and closed in your heart, you will live in a world that might feel like hell.

If you live in a world where you have love, purpose, self-awareness and joy, then it may feel like heaven to you. The idea of eternal damnation and burning in hell is a human idea and nothing to do with me."

Another asked, "In my upbringing I was taught about sin and wrong doing and about confessing my sins. Am I really that sinful and do I need to be forgiven?"

"Maria, that is a very good question. No, you are not sinful. Sin is a human invention. From my view, sin does not exist. There is no need to be forgiven. Humans have gotten confused about forgiveness. Forgiveness is really about changing your thinking about how you judge yourself and others. If you think you have done something wrong, then the most important person to forgive is you.

"Most people live the best lives they can and I applaud your efforts. You were born in the perfection of all that I Am and in a state of grace that is granted by your birth as a living being of the universe.

Someone then asked if Allah and GUS were one in the same.

"Amir, Allah is another name for me. All that is written in the Koran are human words, not mine. That is a holy book because of what those of your faith believe, but it must only be seen as a collection of human ideas. I recommend reading the Koran to everyone who seeks inspiration.

I appreciate the way so many people get together and say my name. It is a very rich tradition, but it is a human idea, not one created by me. Your best prayers are offered in the quiet moments between you and me. Please bring women into equal partnership with you, for they too, are created in my likeness. "

At the end of each discussion GUS reviewed the way for everyone to communicate with GUS quietly one-to-one. It is very simple, GUS said, "if you want to have a relationship with me, all you have to do is ask and I will be there.

"The best way to know me is to let me know what your concerns are and how I can assist you and then wait quietly for my response. The response will always come if you are open to receive it. Open means being willing and in a receptive state.

"In the quiet stillness, I Am always here waiting for you."

The questions came, GUS answered and this went on for 24 hours all over the world. In some places GUS stayed for 3 or 4 hours. In others, especially the small groups, GUS was finished in much less time.

GUS remained for over 12 hours in a large stadium where GUS had promised to stay until the last person's question was answered.

When the time came to an end on this special and transformative day, it was as if the earth stopped spinning on its axis for a moment. There was a sense of a great transition, as if all humans had turned inward and ignited an inner light that would never again go out. No one knew what this would all mean, but they all knew it would be profound.

That day of transformation saw the dawning of a strange new light that seemed to come from a distant star. At night it was seen all over the planet. It was the new star that GUS had brought into the night skies to remind all humans that GUS was there in the dark times as well as in the light.

There were newspaper accounts of GUS's words in every paper on the planet. The news was out and everyone had GUS's message available. All people on the planet now knew who GUS was and how they could have a personal relationship.

Heads of state gathered everywhere to discuss what this could all mean. All the "experts" tried to guess what would happen, but none could know the depth of profound change this day would bring about.

Everyone prepared themselves to see what would happen next. There would be so much to observe over the next several months.

The world, as it was currently known, would profoundly change.

Another noticeable effect was that on Monday, many people didn't show up for work. This put all companies on notice that there was a shift of power happening. Many people in many countries had asked about the power that corporations had over their lives and each time GUS told them that power would shift soon. GUS asked people to listen inward and be guided as to what to do.

CHAPTER 22
—————————

The world meeting day was now behind them. GUS told Fred that keeping the blog going was necessary, for the time being, in order to aid the human transition.

The first blog GUS wrote was about the new star.

"Fred, I think I had better explain the new light in the sky."

"Yes, it would be good to know what is going on and what it means," agreed Fred.

"That new source of light in the sky is a star I moved here from a far away galaxy. I wanted it to shed additional light on earth as a symbol of the renewed light in all beings here. I also wanted it to be a reminder of this day of truth and awakening. The symbolism of the light is about your connection to your higher nature and to me. I Am the light and so are you.

"When you sit in your own light, you are experiencing your divine nature, your likeness to me. Every person on the planet and all living things have light as an essential part of being alive. Please use this star as a daily reminder of your highest nature. This light will shine in the earthly sky from now on.

"Please pass this story along to the young ones, so they too can know the story of GUS's visit to earth to set the record straight. Tell them how the earth was transformed from that visit."

"Thank You GUS, for this powerful reminder. It's up to everyone to see and to reflect about the light within."

"Yes, Fred, exactly. Reflect upon the light that is in each one of you, which is my light also. Remember, you and I are one.

"Fred, I want to also talk about my experience yesterday with all those that I came into contact with."

"Okay, I'm ready," replied Fred.

"Fred, this was a holy connection that you and I were privileged to share with many."

"Yes, it was GUS, a **very** holy experience."

"Please write something for me, Fred."

"Gladly."

"I want to say how deeply moved I Am by the blessing I received from each of you. You have no idea of the power and grace that can flow through you. Most people I met were showering me with love and kindness. That felt wonderful to receive.

"There are some who have their doubts, but they will explore the ideas I shared in their own way. I always appreciate those that question things. It does a mind good to do so.

"I want to state this with emphasis — each of you is a gift to the planet. Settle for nothing less than gifting the world as much as you can with all that you are. Let your light shine and light up every place that you go.

"I also want to add that this is a profound moment in human history and I ask you to be patient with how this all unfolds. Patience is an essential human quality in times of change. Patience is needed because all the systems of life will take some time to adjust to the new human awareness.

"Governments and corporations will all attempt to hold on to as much power as they can. They are only doing what is in their nature and time will alter all of these institutions.

"This does not mean that you can just go to sleep and allow

things to remain out of balance. The part that is so out of balance is this seemingly endless need of many governments and corporations to have power and control over everything and everyone, instead of focusing on caring for the needs of the people. That focus has not worked well for the people or the planet. Change is so urgently needed here. I will help if you call on me to help with these changes.

"Groups can come to me and ask jointly for guidance. If your group is working on a project for the betterment of humanity, please feel free to call me into your meetings. I will usually respond within the hearts of the individuals, but I may at times show up in voice to guide you.

"I share this now because of my own evolution which has been brought on by my time with you here on the planet. I love our interactions and I will continue to have them. My only request is that whatever gets shared in a group gets passed on to others so they too, can be nurtured by my words.

Please use only my direct words and not your interpretations. Your interpretations are for you. I say this to make sure I don't have to come again to set the record straight."

GUS then directed his comments to Fred. "Maybe that idea is transforming because, now that I have come, the record will be clear for everyone to see. I suggest that *The World According To GUS* be turned into a book.

"All the money raised from the sales will go to support a world wide foundation that will keep a healthy dialogue going about the best ways for the human race to continue to grow towards its fullest potential."

Fred said, "That's a great idea about turning your ideas into a book and using the money from sales for a foundation."

"Yes, I think it is too. I want you and Jenny to head that

foundation with her staff as board members."

"I would be proud to and I'll check with Jenny and her staff, but I'm sure they will also be very happy to do so."

"I am glad you are willing to do this."

"Is there more for us to cover today?" asked Fred.

"Not on the blog, but there are some additional ideas I want to share with you. Let's talk about those ideas soon."

"Okay," replied Fred.

"Fred, I am complete for now."

"Good. I am very tired from being on the go with you for 24 hours and I need to go lie down and sleep. I have been on a buzz with so much going on and I think my body is telling me that the time to rest is now."

"Rest peacefully. I will be back tomorrow. Let us talk about the blog and how things are going when we meet."

"See you soon."

That day GUS was called on by numerous people through direct silent contact and requested to participate in several meetings with groups that wanted to ask more questions. GUS was present for their requests and happy to be of service. Those conversations took up most of the rest of the day.

Here are some of the concerns shared and GUS's responses.

"The world we live in has become such a distraction from what gives real meaning to our lives. Would you guide us on this?"

"Yes, I would like to share a perspective in which I see my humans losing the opportunity for a genuine quality life. I suppose you could call it the *entertainment escape*. You all have so many ways to be distracted. It seems like the culture has become one of entertainment. There are movies, sitcoms, reality shows, sports, concerts, video games, gambling and many more.

"Nothing is wrong with any of those activities except when

you give too much meaning to them and that takes the real meaning out of your life. You have been given unlimited inner resources to explore all you can create.

"Entertainment makes you the passive participant and it becomes easy to numb out about your relationships, your work, your feelings, your goals, your passions in life and your purpose. Numbing means you just don't care as much. With the loss of caring your life can only slip into a mediocre existence.

"There are times when numbing out may be what will work for you but given your resources, that is rare. *Checking out* means you don't like what is going on and if you pay attention to your feelings you will see that things do not feel all right. Your feelings give you accurate feedback and will tell you every time whether you are on or off course in your life.

"You check out because you don't want to deal with something, and sometimes it is multiple things that you want to make go away. This never works out because the things you don't want to deal with keep coming at you. This puts you in a situation in which you are not taking good care of yourself.

"Entertainment is a positive thing when needed, but as a way to deal with life, it will leave you very empty inside. No matter if your sports team wins or your favorite contender loses the most weight, these things do not enrich your heart and spirit. What enriches your life is getting out there and living it; pursuing what gives your life real meaning.

"Wasted time is not wrong or bad, just very unrewarding. The more fun choice is to appreciate what is possible in each moment and refuse to settle for less than the best. There is always so much to do. The rest of the time is for enjoying, for just being you in the quiet beauty of each moment.

"Appreciate the quiet moments of loving your partner, enjoying a walk in nature, having a conversation with a close friend, singing along to your favorite song, painting a picture, or writing a story or poem. There is so much to enjoy and it is mostly all free and you get to have fun doing it.

"So, yes, you can have your cake and eat it too."

"Thank you GUS for clarifying these points," responded the questioner.

"You are welcome. What other questions do you have?"

"What happens when we die? Where do we go?" asked another individual.

"You return to me. That is where you go. When you die you are free of your body and you experience yourself more as energy and light. That energy and light returns to its source, which is in union with me.

"The personality that was you in this lifetime is gone but you still have a sense of *you*, more as a member of one big family that loves you just as you are. It is kind of like a homecoming after you have been gone awhile. You return to receive the most wonderful, loving, kind and caring support, welcoming you with open arms.

"After dying you get a great hug from the Universe as you return to unity consciousness.

"Death is not painful but instead feels liberating. You feel glad to be home and surrounded by such unconditional love. There is nothing to fear about death. There is no hell or heaven, just you joining with me.

"Was that helpful?"

"Yes, it feels like such a relief."

"It is a relief to know the truth beyond the fear. What other questions do you have?"

"Do we come back to earth ever again?"

"The personality of you does not come back but the energy that is you does. Let me explain that. You are energy and you have this history — I will call it your *soul's journey*. This soul's journey is about fully exploring your energy's fullest expression.

"Life is not a school of learning but more like a place to play and express who you are. This energy, which is *you,* keeps on coming back to explore new ways of playing and expressing.

"The universe is ever expanding and so are you. Together, the collective *we* and the individual *you* keep on expanding and exploring. There is an ongoing process."

"Am I ever free of this process of exploring and expanding?" queried another person.

"My, you have a thoughtful and expansive mind. Your use of the word *free* in the question is worth talking about. The energetic *you* never feels trapped in a cycle or stuck in a process. You are energy that is **seeking** expansion through the exploration of life. The personality *you* may feel stuck, but that is your ego wanting to have more control over the endless variables. The process of evolution is full of life, passion, aliveness, love, and joy because that is the nature of who you are and who I Am.

"Is that clearer? said GUS.

"Are there other questions you have?"

Someone spoke up and asked, "Tell us about your life and whether you live somewhere."

"Those are two very interesting questions and I don't think I have ever been asked either of them before.

"Well, my life is kind of hard to explain because it is so unlike anything you can imagine. Wait, I take that back. Inside of you is a deep knowing from your connection with me. If you can access that knowing, then you can understand what I am about to tell you.

"I live in all places at once. I have no residence but I do call the universe my home. I guess you could say I own a lot of real estate.

GUS smiled and although they could not see it, they all smiled back.

"This is proving to be kind of complicated. My life is an endless *being awake* to all that is going on everywhere. No, I don't sleep. I do not have a partner nor do I get lonely. I have found since coming here to talk to you and so many others, that I very much enjoy our interactions and will most likely continue meeting with people for some time.

"I don't have a body, so I don't need to take care of it. I have been inside a body and I felt very restricted, but I did enjoy the eating and moving I experienced in this way. I will never take a physical form permanently because I like my freedom to be without limits.

"My interests are centered on exploring the wonderful creations that humans come up with. Technology is so much fun, as is art and design, music and dance and so much more of what humans create.

"My *TV* is watching the people of Earth and the movement of the stars and planets. I don't get bored and I like gaining insights and having new ideas.

"I do visit interesting places like Paris, Rome, Disney World, the South Pacific, the Rocky Mountains, The Amazon, Katmandu and Jerusalem, to name just a few. I have the very best time talking with genuine people like you. It has been my joy to spend this time with you."

"Thank you."

And then, GUS was gone.

The next day GUS met with Fred and got an update on the comments.

"Hi, Fred, before the blog update, I want to tell you about some very interesting interactions I have had since we last met. I would appreciate you sharing them on the blog. These are the questions that were presented and my responses."

(That is how the preceding segment was recorded and presented here.)

"Fred, how are things going on the Blog?"

"Things are going very well with thousands of comments about Your recent meetings and postings. There are some interesting themes arising."

"What are they, Fred?"

"Well, it seems people do not want to go back to jobs that do not treat them well."

"Well, that makes sense to me."

"The problem resulting from this employee walkout is that commerce has slowed down enough to cause some major reactions."

"What are those reactions? Fred, you seem concerned."

"I am, because the people in power are not very happy and things have gotten very stirred up."

"What can the people in power do?" inquired GUS.

Fred replied, "They can do a number of things to try and re-establish control."

"Well, let's talk to the people and make this transition go more smoothly."

"That would be a good idea."

"I can offer some ideas on the blog and encourage patience. I started this process, so I will stay with it until things come more into balance."

"That is what I thought you would say, responded Fred.

"The Blog and your talks have stirred up a lot of people in

much more powerful ways than most would have predicted. The power brokers, as I mentioned, are not happy. The people are happy because they have been given their freedom back and some of them are wanting their total freedom."

"All right, I need to say some things to help the people rein themselves in. I need to also help with the power transition, is that right?" pondered GUS.

"Yes, and I know people want your response because many of the comments were requesting your feedback," explained Fred.

"Are you ready, Fred?"

"Yes, I am."

"I want everyone to know how happy I Am that you are feeling empowered enough to question those in power. This is a positive development for humankind, but some may not fully appreciate the benefits of you asserting yourselves.

"In other words, let us take this slowly so that everyone can work together for the benefit of all. It is going to take some time, and I ask your patience and understanding as this evolves.

"I have two specific messages. One is for those in leadership — please explore with those you lead, ways to decide what might be the best to assist the process during this time of intense interest in change. You are being called on to use your leadership skills to bring out the best in people and to help everyone rise to this important challenge.

"You cannot stop the forces for change, so instead, I invite you to lead them.

"This is an amazing opportunity to make a difference, which I am sure is something you want to do. You have been drawn to power because it appeals to you. There is nothing wrong with that.

"Now use the incredible power of these times to be an extraordinary agent of real change. I know that there are special callings in each of you. Please step fully into all you have to offer. The world needs you to make a positive difference.

"My message to the people is this — please be patient and work with others to be part of the change process for the good of all. Keep your expectations realistic.

"Show up to work and talk with each other and your leaders about how to transition your workplaces into places you value and also how to take ownership for all that you do.

"This will take some time, your efforts, and lots of expansive thinking. It cannot be done in a hurry or by pushing. There is a huge river of change happening and it is important to let things flow, while channeling the energy so as to prevent chaos.

"The forces for change are gigantic but everyone needs to grow into these forces. Thoughtful dialogue and compassionate hearts are needed now more than ever.

"Please keep your hearts and minds open to the best possible directions and solutions. I know that in each of you is a vast inner wisdom that you can contribute to the mix. Please take the time to actively participate from your highest wisdom and your biggest heart.

"I hope these messages are clear. If you want individual guidance please call on me for assistance. I will be there for you and help you with your needs. I will also help you see the larger picture, which I see.

"Fred, how does that sound to you?" asked GUS.

"It sounds just right and I feel you will get a positive response."

After that posting, which all the other papers carried too, things settled down somewhat over the next several days. Leaders began to lead in ways that were uplifting and resourceful, and people relaxed and took a positive "how can I help?" attitude.

The blog comments reflected a desire for people to work together and be supportive and encouraging of the evolving changes.

There were however, forces that seemed not to be pleased at all, and there began a subtle campaign to ignore the ideas of what they called, "This radical point of view of this questionable GUS." Several days passed before Fred reported this development to GUS. GUS knew it was coming from forces that wanted to control the people.

"So, Fred, let me write about this. Are you ready to go?"

"Ready when you are."

"I am a observer of human history, as you well know. Every time in history when individuals or groups have wanted to gain power over the masses, they have used fear tactics. Their major themes are 'don't trust; you need security; protect yourself; there are bad people out there', and more.

"Those who put you in fear have an easy time manipulating you. You can choose to be in fear and follow those seeking to have power over you or you can choose to love and follow your own heart.

"I want to be very clear about this. When your leaders and your government keep on talking about protecting you, it is those leaders and your government that you need to protect yourself from. You do not need to be afraid; there is nothing to fear except fear itself.

"As part of the empowerment of freeing yourself from your own limits and the limits of oppressive organizations, take on your fear and look it in the eye and say, 'I choose to love instead. I choose courage instead. I choose to stand up and be strong. I choose to believe in my higher nature and the higher nature of all human beings.' Those that attempt to control through fear are easy to replace because their stand is one that lacks true courage. Most human beings are so much more powerful than those who would have you cower in fear."

"I trust that will get the point across, Fred. Don't you think?"

"Yes, I do and while you're at it, would you say something about the morally righteous?" inquired Fred.

"Possibly. I am curious why you are requesting that. Actually I know why, but I was more interested in why you think this is important for you."

"Well, my Dad was quite a righteous man who always acted as if he was better than anyone. And yet, behind his act of superiority was a lot of self-doubt."

"You are exactly right. Those that act like they are better than others or act as if they are morally superior are usually hiding something. What they usually hide is their own self-doubt or their own confusion about who they are and what they believe in.

"If someone is going on and on about someone or some behavior they have judged as being not acceptable, it often indicates that they too, may not be far from having that same fault. A good question, if you find yourself very irritated by what someone is doing, is *how is that like me*?

"People who act morally righteous are full of self-pride. This indicates much self-doubt on the inside. The louder they protest their rightness, the more they may have underlying confusion.

"I have deep compassion for people plagued with self-doubt. They have lost touch with their innate wisdom and their connection to me. Self-doubt also means a loss of self-love. That reminds me to talk about the importance of self-love. Humans get such mixed messages about self-love as they are growing up.

"When they are infants and small children they get lots of love. However, as children reach school age, the world becomes less loving as the experiences of life move away from the heart and toward the mind. Self-love becomes a challenge when your peers and the adults are judging you all the time. In some belief systems, young people are actually warned of the dangers of self-love. It is a false belief that there is something wrong with loving yourself. Self-love is the very best gift to give to yourself.

"If you are able to love yourself and accept who you are, then you can be a loving and accepting human being. If you are not able to love yourself, you will not be able to really love others or accept who they are.

"Self-love is one of the main reasons I came to speak to human beings. Much confusion has developed because of dogmatic points of view and conditioning, so as a result, many have lost their inner compass, which tells them what the truth is.

"The value of self-love is one of the most important truths you can experience. I hope this point is clear enough. Self-love is not only a gift to yourself, but to the world. Self-loving and well loved human beings make great citizens of the planet."

Fred spoke and said, "Yes, that point is clear, but keeping the focus on self-love, when many others feel there is something wrong with that kind of focus, may be hard for some people."

"Yes, you are right. Those who doubt the rightness of self-love, most likely are not able to be open to loving who they are. Those who suffer from self-doubt, who think they are not deserving, and who lack true self-awareness, find it difficult to accept and understand others.

"The best approach for ones who care about those challenged by self-doubt, is to continue to love them and accept them as they are. The kindness of unconditional love can help transform even the most ingrained self-doubter. Love can be contagious and spread its light for the benefit of even those struggling with a blocked heart.

"Fred, I think that is enough for today. I don't want to put people on overload."

"I'm ready to relax, too," sighed Fred.

"What are you up to?"

"Jenny and I have dinner plans with her staff and then she and I have a late night date."

"Well, don't be surprised if I show up at dinner."

"Please do," encouraged Fred.

Fred realized he was alone again and he went outside and took a nice brisk walk to refresh himself. Sometimes he got so excited when he was with GUS that he felt the need to go walk off some energy.

What he noticed too, was that after GUS left, he felt present and in the moment, free of his normally busy, distracted mind. He also noticed that his heart seemed totally open as if he was connected to everyone and everything. He had heard GUS call this state, *unity consciousness.*

That night the dinner was no ordinary dinner.

CHAPTER 23

The dinner that evening was at a restaurant run by the husband of one of Jenny's employees. They met there often because there was a nice big side room that was private and conducive to meetings. About an hour into the dinner, most of those that had come started to feel lightheaded and also highly energized. Then a glow of light filled the room and GUS arrived.

Gus spoke saying, "Do not worry, I have filled you all with the light of insight and the energy of your higher nature. I wanted you all to have a beginning sense of what is it like being in my world. Is everyone doing all right?"

Jenny spoke up first and said, "It's as if I have no limits and am filled with such awareness and clarity about who I am and what my life is about."

Another spoke and said, "I feel completely free, as if I could do whatever I want."

Someone else said, "I, too, feel very uplifted and able to do what ever it takes to have the life I've wanted for a long time."

"Fred, how are you doing?"

"Well, this sense of inspiration is one I have been having for awhile since I've been hanging out with you."

"Yes, it is the same one the others are experiencing. Fred, you have adapted well to feeling so good, haven't you?"

"Well, it is not exactly a hard thing to adjust to and I have begun to really relax and enjoy this state."

They all shared a laugh and seemed to allow the joy to expand until the whole room was abuzz with these emotions.

Another person spoke up and said, "I feel like I'm in love, like when I first met my husband."

"Yes, this state of joy you are in is filled with pure love. Those sensations of such powerful and pure love, such as when you first truly open your heart, are the way genuine pure love feels.

"The state of pure love often fades away because the ego gets in the way and protects the heart out of fear. Pure love is always available in each of you if you step past the fear and put the ego aside."

At first some of the staff remained silent and took the time to appreciate their expanded sense. Eventually everyone shared, at least with those close by. Great excitement bubbled forth because everyone understood this heart-filled expansive state would allow each of them to experience more of their higher possibilities.

GUS continued, "I am so happy to be with you. Please let the love and joy deeply penetrate into every cell and particle of your being. The world needs many who recognize and express pure love.

"I have joined you this evening to share in the joy of your further awakening in heart and awareness. I will be going to other groups I meet with and spreading more of this love and joy.

"More and more people will be beacons of light all over the planet that can share and spread love just by being who they are. Thank you all for carrying my light."

They all thanked GUS in unison and it sounded like a classroom of kids responding to a teacher they all loved. Maybe it was exactly that.

The gathering went late into that night. Afterward, people went home and thereafter, they brought light to everyone in their lives.

The next day Fred thanked GUS for blessing everyone with such powerful love.

"You are welcome, Fred. I am so glad to spread my light anywhere people are open to receive it."

"GUS, what would you like to share with the people today?"

"I can see your fingers are awaiting the call to action."

"Yes, they are."

"Today I have a positive message for all those who are trying to make sense of all that is going on inside of them and around the world. I want to emphasize that who you are inside is love.

"You are love that is pure and open. You are love that is joyous and expansive. You are love that understands and is compassionate. You are love that is unlimited and always present. That is who you are and what you have to give to the world.

"I encourage you to find that pure love inside and allow yourself to be nurtured by it, then you can share that love with those around you. Once you feel love totally fill you and those you love, then you can expand the flow and let it fill your community. When the community is aglow with your pure love, then let your giving of love cover your nation and the entire planet. Imagine if you will, that your love is so rich in abundance, that you can share love with all living things on the planet. You are love that knows no limits."

Fred spoke up. "Those are beautiful words GUS, about who we are. I want to print them out and put these words someplace to remind me."

"Fred, you know those words are true because you can feel the love that is realized in you. Others may not have that experience yet, so I have an exercise for my beautiful creations to do to help each one of them find pure love inside and let it spread.

"Here is the exercise:

Find a comfortable place to sit down and feel your breath fill you up and then flow out into the world around you. Take five slow and deep breaths and feel yourself naturally relax.

Now, imagine that you are breathing love from me directly into your heart. That love, of which I Am the source, fully activates the pure love within you. Then, with each breath, you expand the love so that it fills every particle and cell of your body. Take another breath and feel the healing energy of love nurture you at every level of your being.

Then send love to your family and friends and see pure love fill them and bring health and harmony into their mind, body, heart and spirit. Relax and enjoy this love. From there, send love to fill your community and outward from there to spread across the planet.

Next, imagine your unlimited love connecting with the unlimited love of everyone else around the globe. Now, feel this spreading love circling the planet in waves of light, waves of joy and waves of inspiration bringing healing and harmony to all living things.

Do this on a daily basis and feel the world become a healthy, happy and peaceful place."

Fred beamed and said, "I love this exercise and I will do it everyday and feel your love flowing into me and my love flowing out around the planet."

"Good idea, Fred. I hope everyone is as enthusiastic about spreading love."

"They will be as soon as they feel how expansive this exercise can be. I did it while you were having me write it and it felt like something got activated in me that was powerful beyond words."

"That is the power of pure love, my friend," said GUS with a smile in his voice.

CHAPTER 24

The mass transformation was now in full swing. Today was two weeks since GUS had spoken to the people worldwide and much was going on. *The World According To GUS* blog had been buzzing with activity.

GUS felt the need to make sure the message was available to all who wanted to know what had been shared with the world. There were many who were new to this experience of GUS and the blog served as a valuable tool for spreading the word. Those that did not have access to computers were kept updated by newspapers, which since the World Meeting Day, carried all the posted words of GUS from the blog.

Fred reported that those individuals and organizations that had a lot to lose if people of the planet took back their power, continued to try and manipulate others in order to consolidate as much control as they could.

"Fred, I need to address the forces of the ego that is driven by arrogance and the need to be in control."

"My fingers are waiting."

GUS began, "I know, by now, most of you have heard and maybe have had experience with those who want to keep their power and not share it with you or others. People who are this ego-driven and so determined to have control and power have lost touch with essential important human qualities. Here are several causes why some people lose their humanity.

"First, these individuals have lost their touch with their hearts and higher ability to love and have compassion for others. Their minds are operating without connection to their hearts. The heart is necessary to keep you connected to other human beings. When the heart is lost, then you are capable of all kinds of heartless thoughts, rationalizations and actions.

"Those driven by the need for power and control have unchecked egos that lack necessary heart. Mad leaders for centuries have rationalized their heartless actions by thinking they are caring for those that they attempt to control *for their own good*. The delusion of that thinking is only possible if you have lost your ability to know the higher reality of your heart.

"Second, they have lost their humility. Only the humble can grow and learn. Only the humble can see beyond his or her myopic viewpoint. Only the humble can know me. Not because I need you to be humble, but because in humbleness you can know I exist. Only a humble person can see the bigger picture and recognize greater forces at work in nature and the universe.

"The loss of humility gives you an exaggerated belief in your ideas. It sets you on a path that inflates the ego and makes you intolerable of sensible limits. You think you are the only one who knows what is right and no one else does. These are sure signs that you have lost your way and can't even trust your own thoughts.

"Humbleness is freeing and necessary for anyone who cares about what is for the good of humankind. You can find your way to humility by simply feeling the vastness of the love that created the Universe.

"Third, they have lost contact with the higher self, soul or spirit. The human spirit is the life force that guides you. When you lose contact with the spirit/soul, then you often live in confusion.

"Humans in search of power have no sense of their higher self and the guidance of their spirit. They are, instead, run by their rationalizations and the need to be right no matter what.

"Your spirit/soul is the guiding force in you that is in direct contact with me. Honoring and nurturing your spirit will keep you aware of the greater possibilities and potential that reside in you.

"In spirit you are always free, you are eternal, you have unlimited resources to create the life you long to experience. To know your soul and be guided by it is to allow the Divine to bless your life.

"Fred, are you still hanging in there?"

"Yes, I am doing very well and as always, I am very inspired by your words. I have never felt closer to my spirit then I do now. My heart feels wide open and being with you is a very humbling experience. I feel deep respect for all that you are."

"Thank you for all that you have grown into in the last several of months. Your willingness to expand your point of view is exceptional. You are a ready receiver of divine grace," GUS responded.

"I am very grateful for the many gifts of light and insight you have shared with Jenny and me," said Fred.

"Speaking of grateful, Fred, that got me thinking I wanted to share more about appreciation. I want to say thank you for the appreciation I feel from you, Jenny, her work partners and the many others sending such gratitude my way."

"I am ready to begin when you are ready," replied Fred.

"I want to share other ways to develop a relationship with

me. Most people contact me when they want something or want me to help someone. I appreciate their reaching out to me, but I would invite you to communicate with me about your appreciation for the many gifts of each day.

"You get to breathe, eat, talk, listen, work, play, enjoy, participate, laugh and all this goes on while your body purrs along taking care of itself. A talk with me about how much you enjoy even the smallest moments of life is always welcome.

"This appreciation of life brings even more pleasure to each moment. I don't need gratitude, but you benefit from having a grateful point of view.

"You can talk with me when things are really going well or when you are in challenging times. You can talk to me when you need to figure something out or decide which direction to take in life.

"You can call on me to help you when you are starting a project or are involved in creatively expressing yourself. You can call on me to mend a broken heart or to help a wounded relationship.

"Whatever you may need, I can help you find and express all that you have inside of you. When we work together, it opens you to be able to appreciate the benefits of partnering with me. My support as an inner guide can lift you up and take you further.

"All right Fred, that about does it for now."

"Okay, I am off on the road to cover the team for a week's worth of games in other cities. Please come and visit and we can write when you want to. I know most of these cities well and I would be glad to take you on some walking tours."

"I will stop in somewhere along the way. Will Jenny be with you at all on this trip?"

"Yes, as a matter of fact this is the first trip she will take with me in some time. She will join me in Dallas and from there we will go to Orlando and Miami for some games and to enjoy the warmer weather.

"Jenny loves Disney World in Orlando because of all the fun rides. I am not a big ride fan, but I do like to be with her when she is having fun. I have fun, too.

"That might be an enjoyable time for you to join us. We will be playing and having you along will make it even a more joyful time."

"Great idea! I have always wanted to go to a Disney park but never quite knew how to experience it, but now with the two of you, I could feel all you feel and laugh with you. That does sound like fun."

"Okay, I will tell Jenny we may have a visitor. She'll be happy to know that. Oh, by the way, how much longer do you think that you will be staying in direct contact with people through the blog?"

"I don't know the answer. Why did you ask?" queried GUS.

"Well, Jenny and I would like to have a gathering to say how much we appreciate your stay with us. Of course, we will have the quiet time to be with you in the future, but this direct access through words just seems so much more concrete than the words in my head when we talk in silence."

"You bring up a very good point Fred. I need to think about how people can better feel me when they make direct contact. I have learned that some people can know me better through words and sounds, some through feelings and other sensations, and many may need a visual connection, which is not happening yet.

"I will think about how I can represent myself visually. The new star is one way, but something more personal sounds better. Give me some time to figure that one out."

When Fred and GUS met the next time it was in Miami, Florida on the afternoon before the game with the previous year's world champions.

"Hi, Fred."

"Oh, GUS, I'm so glad you came to visit. Our silent visits have been so supportive, but having you where I can hear your voice just feels better to me."

"I understand," said GUS.

"That is exactly why I have been thinking about how I can connect with those that need to see me. These people count on the visual contact to validate their experience. I will work that out with each individual in the privacy of our contact with each other.

"I could be a familiar face, a source of light, a holy monk, a divine mother or whatever best meets the need of those who want to have a visual image of me. I know each of my people well enough to be able to know what would work best for them."

Fred said, "That idea will be helpful for those who need to see in order to experience. Did you want to put that on the blog?"

"Yes, I do, but what I want it to say is that I will make contact with those reaching out to me in whatever way works best for them. I know my people and I will be there for them."

"I am finished with the note for the Blog," Fred said a few minutes later. "Do you have a topic for today?"

"No, I do not. I will either see you later on the trip or when you get home."

"I'll look forward to that," said Fred.

A few days later GUS caught up with Fred back at his home.

"Hi, Fred, how are you doing?"

"I'm doing very well and you?"

"You know me — I am always full of life and love."

"Yes, you certainly are. I've missed seeing you the last few days. Can I be of assistance to you today?"

"Yes, you can. Are you ready to go?"

Fred responded, "Say when."

"Today I want to talk more about why humans have emotions. But before I do, I want to check in with you and hear how things have been going since I saw you in Miami," asked GUS.

"Thanks for asking. The road trip went really well after I saw you. The team won some good games and the way they played was a real pleasure to watch. Jenny and I had so much fun in Disney World and we're sorry you were not able to come."

"Actually, I **was** there, as I am everywhere, and I saw you were doing so well together that I just watched joy and love in action. It was a beautiful thing to watch."

"You were there? You could have interrupted anytime. We would have welcomed you," asserted Fred.

"I know you would have. Only now you know to think of me as always being there. You and Jenny are doing so well and it seems you have worked out the issues from the past that were between you.

Fred agreed, "Actually, it seems like very little work is necessary. Love is a powerful healer. Our love feels greatly expanded and the things that use to trouble us seem insignificant now."

"I am very glad to see that you two have opened to the pure flow of real love. I can tell the love you two share is as good as ever," said GUS with pleasure.

"Yes, our love actually feels better than ever. We still are talking through some concerns we both have but those conversations are going very well. As I said before, what used to seem like significant trouble between us no longer carries much weight. Since you have come into our lives it feels as though Jenny and I have grown past the limited ways we used to be with each other."

"Yes, the purity of your love for each other will easily tackle any trouble you may face."

"Jenny and I hoped you would be willing to bless our coming back together to live in love."

"I have been all along. And yes, I would be glad to be there to bless you two with grace for your new life together."

It was decided then that the three of them would get together as soon as a new home was purchased and Fred and Jenny were ready to move in together and renew the life they had started years ago.

GUS asked, "Why do you want to buy a new house?"

"Jenny and I feel the old house is full of memories that we want to leave behind."

"I understand what you are saying, but you could just as easily forgive each other for the past and move on no matter where you are," explained GUS.

"I know you're right, but we both feel this change is a positive one and actually we both discovered we never did like the old place that much. We thought it made sense to move into a home that we both love."

"Positive change is something I support 100%."

"Thank you so much for all the support you have given us."

"You are welcome," replied GUS.

"Now for today, I would like to talk about the important part emotions play in directing your life. Emotions are neither good nor bad. Emotions are simply a response to what you are thinking about.

"Feelings like anger, hurt, fear, depression and others would most likely indicate that your mind has been focusing on what it doesn't like. Emotions like joy, love, excitement and contentment would tend to indicate that you and your mind are more fully present and appreciative of life.

"I gave you emotions so you can have them as an indicator of how you are responding to what is going on inside and in the world around you. Your feelings always reflect the thoughts you are having.

"There are two basic sets of emotions. One set of emotions is fear-based, and includes doubt, hate, anger, jealousy and other difficult emotions. The second set of emotions is love based and includes joy, hope, freedom, peace and they are the emotions that enrich your life and make it seem worth living."

Fred continued to write as GUS shared his ideas. Later, the blog received many positive comments as those who responded felt they now understood the role of emotions in their lives.

When they had finished the writing for the blog, Fred said to GUS, "The mass transformation is now in full swing and there is even more going on to indicate that. I was wondering ..."

"What is it that has you concerned, Fred?" asked GUS.

"Okay, you always see through my questions, don't you?"

"That is because I see much more than words. I can also see emotions and yes, your thoughts too.

"Well, it seems that corporate influence and power are be-ginning to be tested," said Fred.

"I think that is a positive development. I have watched the development of corporations since the beginning and they began in order to be of service to human beings. Something has gone very wrong, because in many countries people have become more like slaves to corporate domination.

"Corporations say their only purpose is to make money. That is a totally misguided rationalization. Their only real purpose is to serve humanity. There is no reason for corporations to have legal power over individual rights. They only have it because the lawmakers have not done their jobs.

"It is time for the people to take care of that problem by insisting that corporations return to their original charter. Until that is done, there will be no true peace in the world. The pursuit of profit is a very distorted priority on this planet. The people, the planet and all living things are the priority."

"This point of view will cause quite an uproar, said Fred. Do you want me to write this on the blog?"

"No, not at this time. I sense the people will come to this same conclusion. I suspect they are well on their way to those thoughts already."

Fred replied, "It looks like the people have already taken the initial steps by returning to work and making it clear they want their work situations to improve or they will all leave their jobs. This is an example of the people taking care of themselves, much like the unions did in the past."

"Just as it should be, Fred. I am very proud of the courage and determination of the people who want to have the kind of world they deserve. With the corporations in charge, all people could count on was hoping to survive while those in charge put millions into their own pockets. That is not right and it will change because it must."

"There are so many positive things happening. These next few years will cause a huge change for the better for all people. I look forward to seeing how this all plays out. Do you have more insights to share?" asked Fred.

"Are you ready to write?"

"Yes, I am."

"I am concerned about the leadership that is needed in order to go forward. These will be totally new times and a special type of leader will have to evolve. The *approval seeking* political person under the influence of special interest money isn't the type of leader that will take the planet forward.

"What is needed are people who have heart, intuition, analytical skills, positive self-esteem, courage, true wisdom, humility, consciousness and freedom from outside influence. That is a difficult combination to find."

"Yes, it is," agreed Fred. "Where will those people come from?"

"Those attributes are part of the make up of every human being. These new leaders will most likely come more out of self-realization, rather than formal leadership training."

"Is there anything you want to have me write to encourage these leaders to find their way into roles where they can make a difference?"

"Great question, Fred. Please write that I ask all people interested in making a positive difference in the world to take some time to explore how they want to be involved and that leaders are needed with the above mentioned qualities."

"I posted the leadership announcement. I also recommended that they get in touch with you if they want guidance."

"Excellent, Fred."

For the next several months that the blog continued, the people and their relationship with those in power began to significantly shift toward the people being in power, instead of the people being powerless.

The U.S. government and many other nations went through a new election cycle and the voice of the people was heard loud and clear. There was now new, wise and thoughtful leadership in all the branches of government. Several justices in the U.S. Supreme Court stepped down because they felt they had compromised their higher values.

The people also had a much more active role due to new innovations in voting which allowed every citizen to have direct voting power on all issues brought before the Congress.

There was still a lot in the way of change going on, but things were beginning to calm down as most everyone was beginning to learn to trust the process and be patient with the slow but steady changes.

PART 4

The Healing Story

CHAPTER 25

*T*he *World According To GUS* blog officially ended it's regular posting on a spring day in mid April. This is what GUS had to say on that important day....

"Dear, my wonderful and beautiful human beings. It is time I back away from giving my public guidance and end this regular blog posting. I must admit that this is a sad day for me. I have chosen to end it because I have always believed in free will and it is now time for me to back away and allow what has been shared by me to now be explored by you.

"I came to provide some guidance. I am sure that you will now do a fine job guiding your own life. I know you are ready to take this on, because I can feel it in all of you.

"These past six months have been incredible as each of you have claimed who you are with much greater wisdom and heart. The world has needed people like you in leadership for a long time. I came to help make that happen. I am filled with happiness about the job you have all done to start shaping humanity into what it is capable of becoming. The next few years will begin to make all of these changes even more real.

"I want to remind you that my public role is over, but my private role with each of you is always available to you. I am just a short, quiet, still moment away and I always want to be contacted when you have a need. I will be there and I promise to answer. The answer may come through inner messages I send you, through your intuition or through the guiding words you hear from the place in you that is one with me.

"I Am still working with a few groups, which I will continue to do until it is time to move on. The leadership councils in all countries will have me to consult with if I Am requested. These groups are the difference makers on the planet and that is why I Am continuing to work closely with them.

"I Am more available than you probably imagine. Please ask when help is needed or drop by and just let me know how you are doing. You will always find me willing to listen.

The World According To GUS in book form will go on sale next week. The funds created by the profits will go to the Setting The Record Straight (STRS) Foundation, which will be chaired by Fred and Jenny Jacobs and a board of others whom I trust. The Foundation's money will go to support and continue the many new, insightful and positive changes happening now on the planet.

"Your feedback is always welcome and the book will contain the contact information for the Foundation.

"I must say goodbye to you in this phase of my public contact with humanity. I completely trust you to take all of these good things that are happening and continue to help them grow. Every one of you desire and deserve a wonderful life and now you have the momentum to make it happen for all future generations.

"If you need individual guidance, I will be there. My guidance is not always something that sounds easy, but something that feels right and good in your heart and to your spirit. You will know the right way to go because it will feel right deep inside.

"I want each and every one of you to know that you are loved totally and completely just as you are now. Please go forward with renewed heart, wisdom and spirit."

After GUS completed the last blog, GUS and Fred hopped in the car and headed off to experience nature. Fred had requested that GUS come with him to share his two favorite places on the planet.

"First, said Fred, I want to take you to this wonderful hiking trail in the mountains and then for a walk on the beach at sunset so you can experience both of these places through my senses."

"Fred, you don't have to ask twice for us to go to these beautiful sounding places. I Am ready."

"Good, we'll be there in about an hour."

"That is just about the right amount of time, replied GUS. I had some things to talk with you about."

They drove up into the mountains to hike a section of the Pacific Crest trail down from the famous old lodge at Timberline to a lake about four miles away. The hike was rugged, but the day was beautiful and GUS was in awe of the feeling of nature through Fred's senses.

"Fred, I am very impressed by how all the human senses are impacted by being out here in nature. I feel the healing power of nature for the mind, emotions, body and spirit. I have always loved my creations but I have never experienced them in the way that I can by sharing your senses.

"It is interesting that your senses are more nuanced than what I experience. I understand now that my senses tend to be tuned to such a wide band, that I can miss the subtlety of things. This truly is an enriching experience for me to sense all that you sense while taking in the beauty of all of this."

They walked for about two hours. The rich smells, the fresh air, the sights and the living energy of all of life was nourishing to both Fred and GUS.

"Thank you for bringing me here, Fred. You obviously knew there was something I had not fully experienced about nature's qualities."

"I thought you might have never explored this type of place in a human way, which is to breathe in the air, feel the mountain's presence, commune with the trees, smell the life affirming flow of primal nature, and be lifted up by the expansiveness of all this place has to offer. Sharing this with you brings a great joy to me."

"Fred, your words are like music to me when you talk so wondrously about nature. Being **in** nature feels very different to me than experiencing nature as being part of who I Am. I feel me in nature, and nature as a primal force that moves in ways of which I may not yet have become fully aware.

"Please write a note in the blog as a follow-up to my ending words, that I encourage everyone to spend time in nature and even use that as a place to come into contact with me. I would be glad to share nature with every human being."

As they came into sight of the lake, they noticed a small gathering of people. They were friends who had come to be in nature with GUS and Fred. They had all put together a meal of beautiful and tasty foods to share with each other so GUS could also experience the a picnic through their senses. There was lots to eat, much joy and love to share and many words of appreciation for how all of them felt their lives had been blessed.

GUS was touched deeply by such love and kindness.

"This is what makes loving you so easy for me. You are such loving beings. Thank you so much for all your kindness."

The gathering broke up several hours later and Fred and GUS were driven to the trailhead. From there the two of them were heading to the coast with the goal of getting there by sunset.

"Fred, where is Jenny?"

"She will be at the coast. We have a favorite place and we wanted to share it with you and ask for your blessing as we reunite in love for life."

"That is a wonderful idea," responded GUS.

GUS and Fred had a great two-hour conversation on the trip to the coast. Cannon Beach was the destination and Haystack Rock was the place they were to meet Jenny.

At one point in the conversation, it was decided that seeking joy in life was a very good goal.

GUS said, "Life is too much fun to take so seriously. If you allow yourself to enjoy all that you can, life will be full of happiness, freedom and love. I suggest that you look for fun and you will find lots of ways to have it.

"Those that take life too seriously miss out on so much. There are plenty of reasons to have fun and really none that I can think for not having it."

GUS turned to Fred, "This learning to have fun isn't too bad is it?"

"No, GUS, it can be endured," laughed Fred.

They laughed together and the talk went on until they made the turn that said Cannon Beach. The sun was clearly heading to the horizon soon.

"Where is Jenny?"

"I see her over that way," said Fred, as they stepped onto the sand.

"Oh my, this is the ocean isn't it, Fred?"

"Can you smell it?"

"Yes, I can through your senses and in such a rich way. Ah! The cosmic soup. It smells so full of eternal life."

Soon they were with Jenny. Fred gave her a kiss and hug and

GUS surrounded them both with a warm air of love.

"Hi GUS, thanks so much for being here with us. I just got here about an hour ago and was thinking about you. Fred and I have been enriched by you coming into our lives in so many ways."

"It has been my pleasure too, Jenny. I also have been enriched by spending time with you two."

They all watched in silence as the sun set and disappeared. GUS said, "I bless you both in your journey together. Let your hearts continue to expand and your love and light spread across the planet.

"I also want to thank you both for being who you are. I am going to say goodbye for now but I will return soon." And GUS was gone.

Jenny said, "I think GUS understands that this time is for us."

"I do, too. I wanted to hear how GUS experienced the ocean and sunset."

"I am sure if we listen inward later, GUS will tell us."

"Let's do that," agreed Fred.

CHAPTER 26

*T*he *World According To GUS* was out on the shelves of most bookstores around the world within 30 days. Sales figures indicated that many people on the planet bought copies. Those that could not afford the book's price of $5.00 were asked to pay whatever they could.

The STRS (Set The Record Straight) Foundation was created from those funds. One of the uses for these funds was to set up a worldwide network of places for people to get together and talk. These were often established community gathering places or coffee shops. Only now, they had designated areas set aside to encourage supportive and compassionate conversations and the ongoing inner growth of everyone who gathered together.

The locations were linked to each other across the web. People could travel the world and find positive and supportive places to meet others in most communities.

Because of the shifts that were taking place, a connected world seemed essential. Worldwide communication was now free to everyone and travel to anywhere on the planet was made very reasonable for all.

These centers were great resources for all those in need of a place to hang out or have some food to eat. Many people called them "GUS Shops". The "GUS Shops" became the heart center for many and a source of support for those involved in the continual transformation of the planet.

Fred returned to do occasional sports articles once things had settled down. The basketball team and the newspaper implored him to continue writing feature pieces whenever he had the time.

The Foundation, under the direction of Fred, Jenny and their board decided it was important to write the story of GUS's visit and the transformation and healing that was taking place.

Fred agreed to take on the task, but after trying several times to start the project, he realized he felt uncomfortable without his writing partner.

One day Fred decided it was time to push forward and began writing the stories of how humans took the guidance they received in order to heal themselves and the planet.

Fred wrote, "This story began when GUS showed up one day and began to speak through a blogger in order to set the record straight..."

As Fred was writing he felt a presence, an all-encompassing joy fill his being.

GUS was back.

"Hi, Fred"

"I am so glad you are back," exclaimed Fred.

"Why is that?"

"It seems I need you to partner with me on this as you did with the blog. I know I could do this on my own but it just doesn't feel right."

"I hear you, Fred, that's why I showed up."

"Thank you for always understanding."

"I am here at your service, Fred, my dear friend."

"I am deeply grateful, GUS. Together we make a great team and we can do this effortlessly."

"Okay, Fred, let us tell the events in a story form instead of reporting facts and observations. This is a story about every human being coming more fully into the possibilities within them.

"Okay, my fingers are ready. But before we start, I have a question."

"Good, please ask."

"I wondered how it was for you to experience the ocean through our human senses? I told Jenny that I would ask you about our ocean visit the next time I talked with you".

"Fred, just like the mountain experience, I got to sense the ocean and its power through you. I had never known the depth of vitality the ocean had until I felt it through your senses.

"After I left you, I passed through the entire ocean from the North Pole to the South and all in between including the waters of the Equator. The ocean is a whole different world, so full of life that goes unseen. It was a great joy to be in the amazing place that has evolved from the initial seeds of life I planted."

"I would love to know more about that world, maybe someday you will help me experience more of the oceanic world," said Fred.

"I would be glad to assist you in anything. Are you ready, Freddy?"

Chuckling, Fred replied, "You bet I am."

"The story began on a not particularly noticeable day. The planet was in the midst of going for a spin around the sun. The earthly inhabitants all were busy at their tasks. There was a small shaft of light that descended onto the planet's surface and then, there I was knocking at your door and asking if you would come out to play with God."

"Yes. I remember the moment quite clearly as if it only happened a few minutes ago. When you showed up many months ago, I felt like a kid that had found his lost invisible friend."

"I like that image. I am your invisible friend and I am everyone else's, too.

"I showed up and after you quit shaking in your boots, I got you to agree to do the writing for me. As we explored this form, we seemed to get better at it and it wasn't long before we created quite a buzz on the Web and in the world. I have to admit that I liked creating a buzz. After all, that was my purpose."

"Yes, your buzz is still buzzing," replied Fred.

"I am glad to hear that. The buzz got started and people everywhere felt it. They felt this vibrant energy in their minds, warming their hearts, stirring their cells and connecting to their spirits. It was an exciting time for all who tuned in."

"Yes, it was," Fred agreed.

"Fred, I want to remind all who read this and *The World According To GUS* why I always wanted to capitalize 'I Am' throughout my communications via the written word. 'I Am' is an affirmative statement of both my divine nature and yours. Saying, 'I Am' sets up an inner vibration that aligns you with your higher nature and connects you to me if that is what you want.

"This 'I Am' is purposeful in order to continually invite you to the understanding that each person has a spark of life that is tied directly to the source of all light.

"Everyone can now know, if they choose to, that they were created in the likeness of GUS. This feeling of divine unity allows many to open to their potential for GUS-realization.

"In this realization process, an expanded self-awareness of the body's purpose begins to be appreciated. The physical body is the caretaker of all emotions. Expressed emotions keep the body open and alive, while unexpressed emotions close the body down and become places of inner holding. Focusing on the 'I Am' helps release and heal the old holding patterns.

"Fred, I think I had better get back to the story," said GUS.

"Yes, let's do, but that was a very helpful explanation of a useful tool we can all use."

"Fred, the 'I Am' affirmation is very powerful and useful for most any difficult situation."

"Thanks again for spelling this out. I will make sure it gets posted on the blog as a follow up note to the book."

"Back to the story — personal freedom comes through emotional expression. Dancing, singing, and other creative expressions swept the land as the voice and the body were given expression of their full aliveness.

"This buzz of an awakening people had a momentous affect on everything living and everything stuck in limited functioning. Companies, governments, and organizations got a beginning dose of *people power*. The reaction of some of those organizations showed their need to reassert their control. That reassertion would prove powerless in the face of true empowerment.

"In the past, many people had fallen asleep, looked away, rationalized and ignored what was going on, which caused humanity to begin to self-destruct and to do great harm to the planet.

"It seemed that no one was paying attention. Earth was now weeping, people were dying, governments were lying and corporations were covering up the truth. It had become a mess with no one listening to anyone but those buying influence.

"I had to come to set the record straight because life had become so out of balance and so full of unnecessary human suffering. That was not acceptable. I could not watch it any longer.

"The higher human values had been displaced by greedy intentions and misguided rationalizations. There was no one looking out for my people, so I had to say something. Humans deserved so much more than being harnessed as profit-machines.

"My writing spread light and delight for those that sensed that there was a higher way. People were now waking up from a very long sleep. The great human drama of decay had come to an end. There was mystery in the air and vibrant potential for all to explore and realize. Freedom was experienced at levels many had never known and real joy was everywhere.

"The lights came on inside of people. The realization that something better was possible ignited driving inner forces in people everywhere. They now could see clearly in their minds and hearts how things had gone severely off course in so many ways.

"The time had come for a breakthrough or demolition of the barriers that said, 'no, you can't do that'. The people stood their ground and said, 'We have had enough of being stepped on. No one has the right to hold us down'.

"They saw through the falseness of words. They said it is time to stop intimidation, false threats and phony compassion. They declared that they were no longer going to work hard for someone who didn't work equally hard for their well-being and for the good of all of life.

"The spirit of the heart-driven peacemaker and world changer awakened. There was no more passive submission. There was no more listening to fear manipulated rhetoric. Governments continued to play the fear hand, but no one was buying it anymore.

"People stood up and said 'stop your lies and get out of the way, because your ways of governing, your ways of running business, your ways of trying to control are over.' The people are now the governing force in the world."

"Yes to all of this," Fred said. "You are on a roll."

"Yes, I am feeling the flow of energy that comes from my people as they step into their own power. I say their words as I feel their spirit in pursuit of the light of freedom. Human courage is such a force when it has focus.

"Human courage comes from a heart on a mission. Love is so much more powerful than fear. The faint of heart can only lead with words. There is no real passion without heart. There are only words floating on an air of insignificance.

"Truth, courage, heart, purpose, appreciation and creativity are the true driving forces. Fear, greed and power are ultimately empty and lifeless. My people can feel the rightness of these ideas. They don't want phony, they want real.

"I have had enough. They have had enough. So, together, all that matters will continue to change and evolve.

"This is what waking up feels and sounds like. Everyone is feeling alive, joyous, empowered and connected to their hearts and souls.

"The growing understanding and expanding realization of every human being's divine nature is a permanent game changer. With this expanded sense of self, the world becomes manageable and rich with potential.

"Every single human being can do amazing things with their lives if they choose to realize and express their higher nature. Limitless possibilities open the doorways of the mind to believe anything can happen. Being the creator of your life sets you free to go about doing whatever you need to do. Why settle for ordinary when extraordinary is possible?"

GUS paused and said, "I feel like a motivational speaker after hearing what I just said."

Both GUS and Fred had a good laugh. They loved to laugh together because it seemed to encourage even more laughter.

"I think you have a backup career as a speaker if this GUS thing doesn't work out," teased Fred.

They both laughed some more.

They observed that all the structures of society had been shaken by the new sense of the people. The world would be forever different. The signs were very positive for the future.

CHAPTER 27

———————————

Fred and GUS worked together for a short time longer. GUS liked to refer to their joint venture as, "being about setting the record straight, but also about telling the story about the healing of the planet, about the reclaiming of human life guided by higher values and about the realignment of society to reflect a higher level of consciousness. Everywhere, the real story was about people claiming their hearts and living by the higher laws of love and compassion.

"From my view, taking care of the Earth was one of the main priorities of the transformation. The planet needs healing in many ways. For too long people have acted like the planet was nothing more then a supplier of what they needed. This view of the planet's resources was causing greater and greater problems today and for the future.

"This beautiful blue gem has been poisoned by greed and neglect and it is time we set things moving towards great balance and harmony. The healing of the Earth will bring about the return to a healthy place for all living things. The air will be cleaned up so that all future generations will have clean air to breathe. The streams, rivers, lakes and oceans will be taken care of so there is always a rich supply of water. The clean and protected water will also allow the return of an abundance of fish. Abundance will return to the oceans and food sources will be replenished.

"Fred, these kinds of positive and healing changes will be a miracle of human intervention more powerful than any biblical story of my so-called *miracles.*

"Presently, from what I understand Fred, at every functional level on the planet, things are changing for the better. The world is becoming a place for sharing, a place of diversity, a place of compassion, a place of listening and understanding, a place where all life matters, a place where everyone can live their truth and have their own thoughts, a place of joy and thanksgiving and a place of peace."

"GUS, all of this sounds so wonderful and you have captured it so well with your flow of words," exclaimed Fred.

"It does sound optimistic, does it not? All of this positive direction is what I had in mind when I set the evolutionary process into action. My purpose was to cause the realization of all living things to return to their highest level of functioning.

"Humans have been stuck for too long. I came to invite and, if necessary, provoke a shift.

"I did not know at the time what my intervention would do. Now that I see, I Am glad I took a chance and trusted my people to rise to the occasion. They did and are continuing to do so."

"What are the next steps you see occurring to make this transformation complete?" asked Fred.

"I see the people and their world heading in the right way unencumbered by the dysfunction of social structures.

I see technology, unchained by the small thinking of profit-driven research, inventing and innovating in a new and improved world.

"I see that rising awareness and consciousness is encouraging humans everywhere to evolve into even higher forms of human expression."

"That all sounds so hopeful."

"It does," replied GUS. "This is a direct reflection of human beings unchaining themselves from the tyranny of fearful and limited thinking."

"With your help the chains have been removed," said Fred. "What will your role be now? Have you decided what part you want to play from here on?"

"Fred, my role is evolving less and less from direct interventions and more toward being available to individuals that want support. What I would like to do is meet with you, Jenny and her group again soon. Would you make that happen?"

"Sure. Is there an agenda?"

"Yes, there is, but I want to wait to talk about it until we can all get together."

"Are we finished with writing for today?"

"Yes, for now we are."

"Where do you want me to put these new comments?" asked Fred.

"I suggest that you put them in your Foundation newsletter. I trust your readership will appreciate my updates."

"Great idea. I will put them in there today. The newsletter is live on the web and I am sure that people will be glad to read Your latest words."

"What are your plans for this afternoon, Fred?"

"You know me. I plan to do a workout and then spend some quiet time just enjoying the moment."

"I would love to go for a walk in nature with you. The park in the hills will do very well for that."

"You mean Forest Park and maybe the Japanese Gardens?"

"That would be lovely," answered GUS.

"Okay, I will go change into my hiking clothes and something warm. It is supposed to get cold later."

That afternoon they hiked and talked for three hours. Fred loved the time to talk and learn from his friend. GUS loved the time to talk and take in the wonders of the human mind and heart, while enjoying the sensory impact of nature. They returned just as night was descending on this part of the planet.

"Thanks, Fred, for again sharing your senses with me," said GUS. "The woods and cultivated garden were such contrasts and yet they were both full of the vital forces of life. I love how nature has evolved and also, how, when it is nurtured, it also thrives.

"I am grateful for these precious times together with the beauty of the world around us," answered Fred.

"Fred, your work here on the planet has shifted significantly. Your wisdom has grown so much that there will be many who seek your guidance. Please make yourself available to them and I will guide you along the way."

"I am always in your service in whatever form that takes. I fully trust in you and know you will guide me. These days I feel more like a channel of your wisdom, so I do my best to get out of the way."

"I appreciate your expanding wisdom, Fred, and your complete trust in me."

"I am open and feel confident that I can do what is needed in my partnering with you."

"Yes, you can and you will do it well.

"Fred, I will see you again tomorrow. I have a small gathering I want to attend with a group of Tibetan monks. You remember them from the day I addressed the world? They are an inquisitive bunch and I am going back for my third meeting with them. They are all such beautiful souls and I do love to be with them. Someday you must join me in one of our meetings."

"I would very much love to do that, in order to hear what they ask and what consciousness they bring to the planet."

"I will make arrangements for that to happen."

GUS left Fred. In just a brief moment, GUS was sitting amongst his monk friends, all in deep meditation.

They did not speak but all welcomed GUS into their gathering. It was as if GUS was in the mind, heart and every cell of their beings.

The questions were asked in the silence of the monks' minds. GUS's responses were also shared in that silent meditative space.

These monks just hummed along as if they had incorporated GUS without any disruption. This joyous little band of monks was as divinely realized as any humans GUS had met.

After several hours of sharing in thoughts and heart, GUS said, "Thank you for sharing your light with me, my brothers and sisters. I will go now having been enriched by this exchange."

In silent response they said. "Our community of monks and nuns will be light keepers for you on the planet."

"You are already that and I thank you. Your vibrations are lifting up many others."

"Go journey then, enlightened one, and we will look forward to our next direct encounter."

"So will I, my brothers and sisters of light."

As always, GUS was gone in a flash. (What else would the Source of all light be but a flash?)

CHAPTER 28
_____

The meeting with Jenny and crew happened the next evening at the restaurant where they liked to meet. There was much anticipation and GUS did not let them down.

"Hello, my friends, I have come to join you with a special request I have in mind."

Jenny spoke up, "We welcome your light again into this group of humble seekers of truth and justice."

"Thank you, Jenny, and all you precious souls."

"Yesterday I met with a group of beloved monks and nuns and I asked them to *be the keepers of the light on the planet*. They are as close to me as anyone I've interacted with regarding *awakened consciousness*. I do love to be in their company.

"I am telling you about them because I feel the same connection with you on another level. You are all close to me in my heart as 'loving and caring beings.' My request is that you *be the keepers of love and compassionate action*."

A quiet vibration spread through the room. This was a thoughtful and heartfelt group. They only responded when they were clear in their thoughts and feelings. There were no questions at first as they all just sat in silence with the request.

After a few minutes, one of the staff asked what their responsibilities would be as *keepers of love and compassionate action*.

"You would serve as a reminder of my highest law of love, which is compassion and understanding. That may include speaking up when others are forgetting the priorities of love and understanding. It may be that you teach or model these ways of love.

"The important thing is that the world can count on you to take a stand for love. Yes, I know this is a big request but you have the capacity to succeed or I would not have made this request."

A few minutes of quiet passed and then with eye contact and nods from everyone, they all agreed to be the *keepers of love and compassion*.

They ate, talked, and asked questions for the rest of the evening. By the time the evening was over, they all seemed fully ready to do what was required of them.

"Thank you all for taking on this additional task as well as for overseeing the Foundation. These two tasks actually go hand in hand, so my request is more of a fine-tuning in order to help you put your attention where your awareness is best focused."

"Yes," they said, and each one spoke up to thank GUS for enriching their lives in so many wonderful ways.

"You are welcome. Peace and joy to you," and GUS was gone.

The members of the group all left filled with warmth in their hearts and a sparkle in their eyes. Everything seemed to be falling into place.

GUS again did a number of random drop-ins all over the planet. These happenings created quite a stir. The people in attendance were filled with such inspiration that their hearts opened even further. The light and love from these events spread throughout their communities. There was always great appreciation expressed to GUS for blessing their lives in this way.

EPILOGUE

Everyone had changed so much and these changes had a huge impact on humanity and the well-being of the planet. GUS was no longer seen as a *figure in the sky*, but as a real and positive force available to everyone. There was no mighty fearsome overseer, no bringer of illness or suffering but, instead, a welcoming source of love, compassion and creation.

Everyone had, through GUS, a kind, holy and intimate relationship for personal guidance and to encourage their growth and well-being. Those that related to GUS in this quiet way noticed that their hearts opened up to experience more love and joy in their lives.

The shifting of governing structures was now fully under way and the benefits were noticeable almost immediately. The peoples' online voting capabilities allowed everyone to participate directly in shaping their countries' policies.

There was not always agreement on the best direction to take, but most all were willing to support proposals that made sense and followed the laws of love and compassion.

These were times for all the people. The super wealthy shared much of their wealth. Their giving inspired an outpouring of humanitarian compassion and sharing across the planet.

Those that still were afraid were given support to release and find love in their hearts again.

On a global level, there were communications with people all over the planet. Everyone had what they needed. All extremist groups with their threatening ways were made to feel safe by the love and compassion that existed in the global family.

The world had become a loving place, a place where kindness reigned. There was an acceptance and appreciation for all cultures and differences.

The "GUS Shops" continued to thrive as places where people got together and shared and talked and learned from each other. The human family had become a family again and everyone was welcomed to join in.

There were those that kept to themselves and didn't join together with others. They were left alone to be who they were.

Some were deeply spiritual people who had their own ways of knowing GUS. Others were just quiet people who lived in the glory of nature, free of most human relationships.

Still others had a difficult time healing the wounds of past abuses. They had all the healing support they could use, but they chose to work through their pain in their own ways.

Access to higher wisdom was now available to all human beings. Those that wanted to could become students of the wisdom traditions of the world and become teachers of those wisdom traditions.

Many of the former leaders of government, religion, and corporations went through a period of rejection. This was not a rejection by the people but more of a self-rejection. They had come to understand that their judgment had been lacking and many of them had to work on forgiving themselves and finding new ways to make a difference in the world.

Commerce switched from profit motives to meeting the needs of the people. The goal was a zero growth economy that cared for everyone and the planet.

The animals and other creatures entered into a more peaceful interactive relationship with human beings. All living things were given the respect they deserve. Animals as food sources shrank as other sources were expanded.

The people of the planet experienced a wonderful new renaissance of art and creative expression. Painters, writers, designers, musicians, songwriters, dancers and more, all had the resources to fully explore their expression. The times were rich with creative expression of all kinds.

Everyone benefited from taking in all the great works of creativity in their newly liberated societies.

All were now free to express themselves as fully as possible. This had been the goal when *The World According To GUS* had come into existence — when GUS had come to set the record straight.

Peace and joy for all became the way of the world.

As GUS says, "I knew it would all end happily ever after. Breathe, be present and love"

Fred seemed to speak for everyone when he said, "Thank you GUS, it has been a wonderful journey with you. I'll see you in the quiet spaces of my mind, body and soul."

A NOTE FROM THE AUTHOR

This book was inspired and came through me as a flow of energy and love. I only know this higher being through my own seeking of the truth. I invite each of you to know *the source of all love* in your own way.

Light, love, joy, and peace to each of you that is always found in the presence of every moment.

Joseph